KINKY FRIEDMAN

Spanking Watson

ff

faber and faber

First published in the USA in 1999 by Simon & Schuster
First published in Great Britain in 1999
by Faber and Faber Limited
3 Queen Square London WC1N 3AU

Printed in England by Mackays of Chatham plc, Chatham, Kent

A CIP record for this book
is available from the British Library

ISBN 0–571–20167–9

2 4 6 8 10 9 7 5 3 1

ACKNOWLEDGMENTS

On a trip to the moors, Holmes and Watson were lying in a field looking at the stars.

"Let us test your observational powers, Watson," said Holmes. "What do you see?"

"I see the stars in the beautiful summer sky," said Watson. "What do your observational powers tell you, Sherlock?"

"My observational powers tell me, Watson," said Holmes, "that someone has stolen our tent."

Spanking Watson

"When I'm a veteran with only one eye
I shall do nothing but look at the sky."

—W.H. AUDEN

"A large mammal appears to have passed this way recently."
—DR. WARREN BACHELIS

"You never marry the person you first see Casablanca with."
—KINKY FRIEDMAN
(ON LOAN FROM KACEY COHEN)

I

I T was Monday morning, and the cat and I were staring sulk-ily upward into the moon-sized crater in the ceiling of my loft. Indubitably, it had been the result of the constant pounding on the floor above by Winnie Katz and her lesbian dance class. The previous morning, after attending services at the Church of St. Mattress, I'd finally gotten Rambam on the blower and he'd promised to call Joe the Hyena to round up several handpicked members of the International Brotherhood of Electrical Work-ers. Rambam also promised that he and the workmen would show up this morning at eight o'clock sharp. It was now ten-fifteen and there was no one in the loft but me and the cat.

"It's a shame what's happened to the glorious tradition of unions in this country," I said to the cat. "We've gone from leg-endary leaders like Joe Hill to modern-day mob leaders like Joe the Hyena. Of course, without Joe the Hyena we wouldn't be currently receiving the help we're currently not receiving. What would Woody Guthrie or Tom Joad have to say about all this? At least we can thank the Baby Jesus that lesbians don't have unions. We'd never get this damn ceiling paid for."

The cat absorbed my comments in a state of stoic silence. The cat was a Republican and had never cared a flea about the problems of the working man or woman in America. I, on the other paw, had a great deal of sympathy for the plight of the working person. It couldn't be said that I had a great deal of *empathy*, however, seeing as I'd never worked a day in my life unless, of course, you wanted to count my two years in the Peace Corps, where I labored rather fruitlessly in the jungle teaching people who'd been farming successfully for over two thousand years how to improve their agricultural methods. The only things that came out of all the time and effort I expended there were a large harvest of tedium, a tattoo, a handful of friends I'll probably never see again, two blowpipes gathering cobwebs on the wall, and an occasional late-night craving for monkey brains. Some would say that's pretty good for eleven cents an hour.

"Monkey brains," I said to the cat, as I drew my second cup of espresso, "are considered quite a delicacy by the Punan tribe of Borneo."

The cat wrinkled her nose slightly in a moue of distaste. She followed this patrician behavior with a barely audible *mew* of distaste. Like many cats, and many Republicans, she was extremely ethnocentric. Her attitude toward the Punan tribe of Borneo might be effectively summed up as: "Let them eat monkey brains."

Just to irritate the cat, I stayed on the subject a little longer than was probably necessary. I lit a cigar and, with a certain professorial detachment, watched the fragrant blue smoke billow upward into what used to be my ceiling. Then I continued, undeterred, with my anthropology lecture, which I could tell was starting to make the cat want to climb a wall. If the truth be known, it wasn't all that exciting from my side of the lectern either, but if you're waiting for Rambam and the International Brotherhood of Electrical Workers you've got to pass the time

2

女 women, childhood, and various other lost opportu-
e, cats usually come back from wherever it is they go.
lid, not surprisingly, at just about the time my two
rkmen sat down at the table and started taking out
Probably because Joe the Hyena had selected them
they did not exhibit what I suspected might be a
ory brand of behavior reserved for other "jobs." In
haved like two happy-go-lucky Italians, offering to
atered sumptuous Little Italy–style lunch with me
Both of us, of course, accepted. It was an offer we
se.
d as an amateur private investigator had been
tely and my social life had been a bit sluggish as
because the architecture of my personality was so
most people never got past my first three minutes
harm. I kind of liked it that way. It saved me from
dependent, long-term relationships. So I was not
to Vinnie and Gepetto's sharing the lonely loft
he cat for a few days. Superficially, they were

somehow or you'll inevitably become highly agitato, then you'll
snap your wig, then you'll hang yourself from the nearest passing shower rod, then you won't ever have any problems with
your ceiling again because your floor will be the sky.

"The Punan tribe of Borneo are nomadic pygmies," I continued, "who by this time have no doubt been displaced by some
totally unnecessary government dam or have ceased to exist entirely because some Japanese lumber conglomerate has cut
down all the trees. No trees, no monkeys, no brains, no Punans.
The only anthropological relics of their existence, indeed, may
be these two blowpipes one sees exhibited upon this wall."

As I turned to direct the cat's gaze to the wall in question I
observed a rather curious scenario. There were not only no
trees, no monkeys, no brains, and no Punans. There was also no
longer any cat.

Fighting down a mild panic, I had just begun to start searching for the cat when a noise that sounded like a foghorn from a
large ship at sea drifted ominously into the loft. I walked over to
the kitchen window and shoveled a glimpse four stories down
at Vandam Street. It was pretty foggy out there and I couldn't
see the ship. No trees, no monkeys, no brains, no Punans, no
cat, no ship, no ceiling. Have a nice day.

The foghorn sounded again, and this time I flung open the
window to the arctic void that was New York City in February
and noticed a rather nondescript van parked on the sidewalk
somewhere in the middle of a necklace of garbage trucks. The
van began spitting out several little stick men and one of them
appeared to be beseeching me from the street.

"Throw down that fuckin' puppet head!" shouted Rambam.
"I'm freezin' my ass off down here!"

I wandered over to the refrigerator and plucked from the top
of it the last cheerful face in the city. The face belonged to a little
wooden puppet head, and nobody knew where the puppet itself
was now. Very possibly its strings were currently being pulled by

a crippled ballet dancer on the seventh ring of Saturn. But as far as the head was concerned, it was still smiling, even with the key to the building wedged firmly in its mouth and a brightly colored parachute attached from the place where its neck would've met its body. I threw the little head out the window and watched it float gracefully down into Rambam's rapacious hands. Then I closed the window before my own neck froze off my body and somebody tied a brightly colored parachute to my scrotum.

"Come out, come out, wherever you are," I chanted loudly, "or I'll puff on your whiskers with my big cigar."

The cat and I did not enjoy a particularly healthy or mature relationship, and certainly the cat did not come out from wherever the hell she was. In a state of high exasperation I gazed up at the ceiling, and that brought me back to the situation at hand. This was hardly the time for a game of cat and mouse. Winnie Katz and her lesbian dance class had done severe damage to the ceiling of the loft and, to add insult to injury, Winnie had refused to take any responsibility or to help pay for the necessary work required to fix it.

"One man's floor is another man's ceiling," I'd told her rationally over the blower.

"It's one *person's* floor, cowboy," she'd said. "And there's nothing wrong with my floor. Your ceiling is structurally weak."

"Right," I'd said. "And how many lesbians do you think can dance on the head of a pin?"

"I wonder how many can dance on top of your pin*head*?" she'd said, and hung up the blower.

No doubt, I'd sort out the cat and the lesbian situation later, I figured. I could hear Rambam and the workmen coming up the stairs, and with any luck they'd be on the job soon. The ceiling did look structurally weak, actually, and besides, staring at that yawning chasm was beginning to give me an empty feeling. Like I'd been living on this planet for fifty-three years and all I had to show for it was a hole in the ceiling.

"Joe sends his best," said Rambam, w
with the puppet head in his hand. "He al
Gepetto."

"Jesus Christ!" said Vinnie, as I startec
"Who the hell lives up there? A fucking e

"A lesbian dance class," I said.

"Dat explains it," said Vinnie. "What t

"Ten-thirty," I said. "But it's no probl

"All day?" said Vinnie. "You gotta b
all week."

"Sorry we're late, by the way," said
by da fish market to—uh—take care of
ing. Shit, man, dis looks like a big jo

"Joe told me he'd give Kinky the
bam.

"I know," said Gepetto, "but he
ceiling was big enough to hide Jir

"I'll talk to Joe again," said Ra
run. I've got to pick up a delivery
You guys might as well get start
the meantime, ask Kinky if ther

"Hey, Kinky," said Vinnie,
stairs, "dere is one thing we m

"What is it, Vinnie?" I said.

"Mustard," said Vinnie. "It'

U NLIK
nities in li
This one
Italian wo
their lunch
for the job
more unsav
fact they be
share their
and the cat.
couldn't refu
My caselo
rather light la
well, possibly
repellent that
of superficial
destructive, co
entirely averse
with me and t

quite passable company. Maybe superficial was all there was.

I therefore resolved to treat them like any other housepests. They were certainly not as tedious as some visitors I'd had—Ratso, for instance. Thus it was that I offered them both a cup of espresso after lunch, poured from the ornate, commercial-sized espresso machine with the eagle on top that took up about a third of the kitchen. When Vinnie and Gepetto got a close look at the espresso machine they became more animated than at any time during the course of our short relationship.

"Where'd you get dis?" asked Vinnie.

"Joe sent it to me years ago."

"Why'd he do dat?" asked Gepetto.

"I think because I once saved his daughter from a mugger in a bank on Christopher Street."

"It's a beautiful fucking machine," said Vinnie.

"It's a good fucking story, too," said Gepetto. "But it ain't true."

"What do you mean?" I said.

"Joe ain't got a daughter," said Vinnie.

I thought about it as the three of us sipped our espresso in stony silence. I hoped Rambam would get back pretty soon so I wouldn't wake up from a power nap with the cat's head in my bed. The cat, for her part, seemed to be genuinely warming up to the idea that we'd be having company for a while. When Vinnie and Gepetto finally began setting up some ladders, she took up her place in the rocking chair and settled in for the show. I walked over and sat down at my desk and wished I'd had the forethought to hire Bob Vila.

What the hell, I figured, when Rambam gets back we'll get this little misunderstanding all sorted out. Either Joe the Hyena had a daughter or he didn't have a daughter. All I knew for sure was that I had an espresso machine and these guys were probably jealous. No doubt it was a common Italian affliction. Espresso-machine envy.

But I wasn't really very upset with the two Italians. I wasn't even that irritated about the five-foot-wide hole in the ceiling. What I was still rather highly agitato about was the fact that most of the plaster that had once been inside that hole had fallen directly on top of my head.

According to Stephanie DuPont, the drop-dead-gorgeous blonde who lived upstairs across the hall, I'd only been unconscious for a few hours. She's the one who found me lying on the floor of the loft feeling like Rip Van Winkle on gorilla biscuits. What'd been two hours for her had seemed like twenty years to me and I still wasn't sure that we'd circumcised our watches. The blow on the head had sent me reeling back to Ratso's skid-marked couch, my first official lodgings in New York. If it all had been a dream, I wanted my money back.

Nightmare was a better word for it. Nightmares always seem to have a longer shelf life than dreams. They reach more people. And while many Americans may well have forgotten many of their dreams, the stuff of nightmares is something you never totally shake off until you fall through the trapdoor. In my case, I'd just lived twenty years of hell in approximately two hours, and every single damned waking aching moment of it, I reflected as I took a fresh cigar out of Sherlock Holmes's porcelain head, was Winnie Katz's fault.

Now, oblivious of the workmen and the world as well, I lit the cigar with a kitchen match, always vigilant about keeping the tip of the cigar ever so slightly above the tip of the flame. As I watched the smoke drift upward toward the ravaged ceiling, my damaged dreams drifted right along with it. "His Kinkyship sails at dawn," I said to the cat.

The cat, of course, said nothing. She was still riveted to her rocking chair, watching two men fixing a hole.

Rationally, I knew that even Winnie Katz had not been diabolical enough to deliberately cause the plaster to fall on my head. That having been said, because of one spiritually lackadaisical lesbian, I was forced to suffer and relive twenty years of Peruvian marching powder–induced limbo in which I had found myself stalking a psycho who was busy stalking my fugitive friend Abbie Hoffman, who'd gone to Jesus almost ten years ago. Raking the dead leaves of the past is evil yard work. Whether you do it for two hours or twenty years, it leaves you feeling deader than the leaves you rake.

Vinnie and Gepetto were long gone by the time Rambam returned to the loft. The cavern in the ceiling looked exactly the same as it had before he'd left. The only difference was that now the loft had taken on the dark ambience of an abandoned construction site in the Bronx, with ladders, scaffolding, tarps, and equipment strewn all over the living room.

"What do they think this is?" said Rambam. "The fucking Sistine Chapel?"

"You're the one who picked these guys."

"I didn't pick these guys," said Rambam with some heat. "Joe the Hyena picked these guys."

"Which brings us to another little problem," I said. "Does Joe the Hyena have a daughter?"

"Does Joe the Hyena have a daughter?" asked Rambam incredulously. "Does the Pope wear a humorous-looking hat? Of *course* Joe has a daughter. That's why he sent you the espresso machine. You rescued her from the mugger at the bank, remember? Or have you finally burned out your remaining brain cell?"

"Vinnie and Gepetto say: 'Joe ain't got a daughter.' "

For once I'd said something that seemed to stump Rambam. Almost robotically, he poured a shot of Jameson Irish Whiskey into a nearby glass, took the glass with him over to the window, and silently stared out into the darkening street. Desiring to stay on the same wavelength, I poured a liberal portion of Jameson's into the old bull's horn that I often utilized as a shot glass and proceeded to drain its contents down my neck. I waited for Rambam to say something, but evidently the cat had gotten his tongue.

"What do we do?" I said at last. "How do we check something like this out?"

"Very carefully," said Rambam.

3

As the days passed, Vinnie, Gepetto, the cat, and I became almost a little family. We took countless espresso breaks, we looked forward to having lunch together, and on Thursday, when the two workmen took a holiday for Mussolini's birthday or something, the cat and I actually started to miss them. Possibly the presence of other human beings had merely underscored the abiding loneliness of life in the loft. Maybe it was just the estrangement in the soul of the private investigator as he forever futilely attempts to solve the mysteries of life in the big city.

At any rate, the work went on at about the pace of a garden slug tediously traversing a giant sunflower. There were, of course, moments of humor, like the time the lesbian dance class started up just as Gepetto was on top of a ladder preparing to apply some plaster. As he was getting ready to make contact with a damaged area, more plaster came raining down on his face giving him the countenance of an angry Italian mime artist.

"Goddamn gap-lappers!" he shouted. "Kinky, man, you gotta do something to stop dis shit or we're gonna be losin' ground."

"I'm calling her every day," I said. "What else can I do?"

"You want we should *do* something?" asked Vinnie, with a sudden childlike, evil earnestness that was rather unsettling.

"No, no," I said. "I'd rather stick with the diplomatic route in dealing with these damn lesbians."

"Then watch what you guys say about lesbians," Vinnie shouted from the top of his ladder. "I like pussy, too!"

Everybody laughed except the cat, of course, who stared straight forward rather balefully from the kitchen counter. For a great many reasons she found little if any humor in the remark.

By the time Friday morning rolled around, I was chagrined to wake up and find all the plaster that had been applied on Wednesday, before Mussolini's birthday or whatever it was, once again lying on the floor directly beneath the hole.

"Maybe we *are* losing ground," I said to the cat.

The cat, of course, said nothing. She was sitting on the windowsill awaiting the arrival of Vinnie and Gepetto.

"Rambam has assured me that we *will* get the Israeli Discount for the work and that's a good thing because at the moment we're not exactly fartin' through silk."

The cat looked back at me with a brief glance of disdain. Like all cats, she was essentially a humorless, constipated prig at heart, if indeed, cats had hearts. Like all people, I was essentially perverse, pugnacious, paranoid, covered in the grime of humanity, and always and forever standing in the way of myself and my heart, if indeed, people had hearts.

"I know you must think me frighteningly homophobic, but those damn lesbians have already taken away two hours of my life and sent me back twenty years to a living hell. Not to mention the hell I go through listening to whatever they're doing up there."

Almost like a sign from the heavens, the thudding and crashing sounds of the lesbian dance class started up again directly over our heads. Possibly it was the slight hangover I was currently experiencing that caused the noise to seem even more intolerable than usual. The cat looked over at me with her traffic-light eyes, and if I hadn't known better I could've sworn that she was smiling.

"Mark my words," I said grimly. "This goddamn racket's going to stop or I'm going to—"

I never finished telling the cat what I was going to do about the racket upstairs because our senses were now being visited by a racket from the street. Walking over to the window, I observed that Vinnie and Gepetto had navigated their van through a phalanx of parked garbage trucks and now stood on the sidewalk screaming for the puppet head. I went over to the refrigerator and saw that the puppet head was still smiling at me. I did not return the smile. I picked up the little head, opened the window, and tossed it out onto the frozen tundra of Vandam Street.

Vinnie and Gepetto both grabbed for the puppet head at the same time, causing Vinnie to trip over the curb and Gepetto to slip on the icy sidewalk. It's a good rule never to laugh at falling Italians, especially if they work for Joe the Hyena, so I didn't. I did take some bitter pleasure in watching the little puppet head crash heavily onto the sidewalk between them.

"That ought to wipe that sick, wooden smile off your face," I said.

I felt remorseful almost immediately. What in the hell was happening to me? It's an unfortunate state of affairs when a little black puppet head has become your best friend in the world, but that had been the situation for some years now. And here I was letting Winnie Katz and her godforsaken, heathen crew put a wedge between one of the most durable and heroic friendships of my life.

"I love that little Negro puppet head," I said to the cat, "and as far as I can tell, he loves me. May he continue to smile that brave, stoic smile until all the pigeons in New York fly away to Hawaii. Forgiveness is the ornament of the brave."

The cat looked at me the way you look at a person you've just discovered is a former mental patient. The pity in her eyes was almost suffocating.

"May the puppet head smile until all the cats in New York fly away to Hawaii," I said.

The cat, of course, said nothing. There wasn't a hell of a lot to say, I suppose, and if anybody'd said it, it wouldn't've been heard anyway because of the lesbian dance class.

I'd recovered my composure a bit by the time Vinnie and Gepetto walked in, and I took the little puppet head and placed it carefully, perhaps even affectionately, back on top of the refrigerator. Its eyes were black and clear and its smile constant and true.

"Welcome home," I said. "How was the trip?"

"What'd you say?" shouted Vinnie.

"Nothing," I said, slightly rattled. It's one thing to have someone overhear you talking to a cat, but it's quite another to be overheard carrying on a conversation with a little black puppet head.

"You can't hear a fuckin' thing in here," shouted Vinnie, gesturing obscenely toward the ceiling. "How long's dat pounding been going on?"

"As I've stated before," I said, "Winnie Katz's lesbian dance class is like God. Mankind never sees it, but you always know it's there."

"Heavy," said Gepetto.

4

LATER that afternoon, with the garbage trucks growling outside the windows, the lesbians banging and thudding relentlessly from above, and Vinnie and Gepetto hammering, chipping, and scraping away from below, I finally managed to get Winnie on the blower.

"What now?" she shouted, after I'd identified myself.

"If you don't have the decency to return my messages," I said, opting for a rational, mature approach, "at least have the decency to refrain from that infernal pounding until I've had the chance to get my ceiling repaired."

"How *dare* you!" she screamed. "This is my *livelihood!* This is my *work!* I don't sit around on my ass all day smoking a cigar and playing private detective. This is my *art!*"

"Okay, don't get your feathers ruffled. I asked you politely and you turn into a drama queen and try to bite my head off."

"Not queen," she said. "Queens are the guys. You probably have other names for them."

"Critics," I said. "We call them 'critics.' "

"Well, the critics have raved about my work. The *Times* gave me a brilliant review for my most recent dance performance."

"What was it? *The Nutcracker*?"

"Funny."

"So you'll give it a rest for a while? Let the workmen finish the job?"

"Are you kidding? This is a dance rehearsal. It wouldn't stop if the sky was falling."

"That's what I'm trying to tell you. The goddamn sky *is* falling."

"So's your erection, Chicken Little. Hit it, girls!"

Just before she hung up the phone I heard the music start to blast again and about two beats later the thudding on the ceiling recommenced and the whole loft seemed to be vibrating like a tambourine.

"You whore!" I shouted into the dead blower. "You mean-minded, vacuous bush pilot!"

"That's tellin' her, Kinky, man!" shouted Vinnie. Gepetto banged his trowel against the top of his aluminum ladder in a show of support.

"Kill them lesbiterians!" he shouted.

The cat looked up at the ceiling. Then her eyes changed from yellow to green and she stared straight into my soul with a gaze of frozen feline feminine fury. It wasn't hard to surmise upon which side of the ceiling her sympathies resided.

That night the living room of the loft looked like a city after a war. The cat and I were the only inhabitants of that desolate city within a city, and we knew that somehow we had to sustain ourselves. The cat, apparently, was finding my personal holy war against Winnie Katz to be quite a traumatic experience. She ate a rather large amount of Southern Gourmet Dinner that several days later Vinnie had to scrape off the inside of his toolbox in the form of dried cat vomit bearing the distinct shape of General Augusto Pinochet's mustache. As for me, I smoked an endless chain of resurrected cigars, paced an endless corridor of narrow walk space back and forth across the living-room floor, and made an endless succession of fruitless phone calls in an effort to find a living soul in New York to help me feel sorry for myself. I also drank enough Jameson Irish Whiskey to render me fundamentally out where the buses don't run.

The Village Irregulars, as my loose-knit circle of faithful friends had come to be known, did not seem to be accessible that fateful Friday night at Cinderella time. Ratso, my flamboyant flea-market friend, a creature of narrow habit, was out playing his ritual late-night hockey game. McGovern, my favorite Irish poet and intrepid reporter, at this moment, was no doubt drinking a tall Vodka McGovern, possibly at the Corner Bistro, possibly at the Monkey's Paw. Mick Brennan, world-class photographer and troublemaker, was probably in the darkroom masturbating like a monkey or else out on the town demonstrating why some people called him "the Poison Dwarf." Rambam was on some mysterious stakeout and wouldn't have responded if you'd told him that somebody'd barbecued his grandmother. Stephanie DuPont, the object of my broken American dreams, was no doubt on a date with some thirty-year-old investment banker with a three-inch dick. The only one who seemed to be home was me and sometimes I wasn't even too sure of that. Home can be a pretty tedious place if you're not far enough away to begin to start to miss it.

" 'The fight is not going to be with the world,' " I said to the cat, " 'but with yourself.' Stephen Crane, 1896. For those of us who slept through all their classes, he wrote *The Red Badge of Courage*."

The cat was currently sleeping under my desk lamp which she often commandeered as her private heat lamp, much to my irritation on the rare occasions when I had any work to do there. If you're a good private investigator, you don't really need a desk, except without a desk you wouldn't have any place to prop your feet when you're waiting for a case. My feet were currently propped up on the desk, my hand was wrapped around the old bull's-horn shot glass, and my bloodshot eyes were trying to determine if any cliff dwellers possibly could've lived in the archaeological ruin that I'd once looked up to as my ceiling. The cat continued to sleep.

"Emily Dickinson died in 1886," I said. "Her only friend was her dog named Austin."

The cat continued to sleep. Her left ear, however, appeared to twitch briefly but rather definitively, as if in mild irritation or vague displeasure. Possibly there was a flea in her ear. Possibly it had fallen out of the hole in the ceiling.

"F. Scott Fitzgerald was born in 1896. He was not a particularly happy American either. Ernest Hemingway made fun of his relatively small penis and he was broke most of the time and plastered all of the time. Possibly with the plaster from the hole in the ceiling. He died a lonely death in Malibu, which is not as romantic as dying in the gutter but is a good place to live if you don't mind paying a million bucks for a beach-front house that looks like somebody's garage door."

I was starting to get seriously monstered and the cat was not responding to therapy and the hole in the ceiling appeared to be growing almost as large as the hole in my life. But I lit a fresh cigar and poured a fresh shot of Jameson's into the bull's horn and started writing rather macabre, threatening notes to Winnie Katz on my Big Chief tablet. I didn't need anyone to tell me that it wasn't healthy to carry on a conversation with a sleeping cat. Fortunately, there wasn't anyone there to tell me.

"In 1889, Father Damien died amongst the leprosy victims of Molokai. Van Gogh croaked himself the following year. Two years earlier, he'd worn a hat with burning candles on it to paint *Night Cafe* and *Starry Night*. There was nothing wrong with that. And around that time Oscar Wilde was tried and convicted of sodomy. The charges were later reduced to following too closely, but by then the damage had been done. He went to

Jesus in a night cafe very similar to the one Van Gogh had painted with candles on his hat. And Damien was a carpenter just like Jesus. I wish those guys could've gotten together and been friends during the flying hours of their madness. Perhaps they did. But like a sleeping cat, the world let them slip away to the stars."

I killed the light and, like the cat, I went to sleep.

5

I woke up Saturday morning with an extremely unpleasant hangover and somebody pounding on the door of the loft. Even in my semiconscious dream state I had a pretty good idea who it was.

"Kinkstah! Hey, Kinkstah! It's me, Kinkstah! Open up!"

Clearly, it was Ratso. The only thing that remained unclear was how he'd gotten into the building without the puppet head. Still wearing my Borneo sarong, which resembled a childhood backyard tent because of my morning monstro-erection, I stumbled to the door, quoting everyone from Shakespeare to Charles Bukowski on the way. Ratso wasted no time rushing into the place, rubbing his hands together like an insect, and observing the war-torn landscape of my living room.

"Hey, Kinkstah!" he shouted in a rodentlike voice that was loud enough to hurt me. "You didn't tell me you were putting in a skylight!"

I sat down slowly and held my head in my hands. I closed my eyes, saw a few of Van Gogh's stars, and made a fervent wish that Ratso would go away. But it was not to be.

"Great idea, Kinkstah! Get a little light in the place."

"Ratso," I said, "we're on the fourth floor. This is a five-story building. How in the fuck am I going to put in a skylight?"

"It's not going to be easy," he said.

"No, it's not."

"Then why are you doing it?"

"I'm doing it sort of as a conversation starter so if people come over and wake me up early on Saturday mornings there won't be any lapses in social etiquette. I'm also hoping that because of the depleted ozone layer, the skylight will magnify the sun's harmful rays in such a way as to do serious harm to anyone who comes in here and asks stupid questions. Speaking of which, how'd you get in the building?"

"A passing lesbian held the door for me," said Ratso. "Very courteous. Kind of cute. Friendly."

"Why don't you ask her out?"

I walked over to the espresso machine and jumpstarted it into life. Moments later it began gurgling, hissing, and humming a pretty decent approximation of "England Swings" by Roger Miller. The sound of the espresso machine and the momentary silence from Ratso was already making me feel much better. "England Swings," of course, had been Rita Jo's and my song many years ago, when we'd traveled to London together. Rita Jo had been Miss Texas 1987. And, as my friend Don Imus often points out, I was Miss Texas 1967. I'd talked to Rita Jo several days before and told her how much I still loved her. "There's a hole in my life," I'd said, and I hadn't been referring to the roof. "Why don't you stick a cigar in it?" she'd suggested. Nothing lasts forever, I thought, as I drew two cups of hot, bitter espresso. Not even "England Swings."

"Okay," said Ratso, "so you're not putting in a skylight. That leaves only one other possible explanation for what you could be doing here."

"And what would that be, my dear Ratso?" I said, handing him a cup of espresso.

"Performance art," he said.

Ratso sat down on the davenport and adjusted his coonskin cap with the little creature's face sewn on the front of it. He was wearing his lox-colored slacks, red antique shoes that had once belonged to a man who had stepped on a rainbow, and a phlegm-colored cashmere sweater that might've been rather fashionable-looking had it not had written across the front of it the inscription "Die Yuppie Scum."

I took my leave of Ratso momentarily to go into the bedroom and change into something slightly less prurient myself. The cat was just waking up, and the sight of Ratso sipping espresso on the couch was not a crowd-pleaser for her. Ratso had never done a thing to the cat, yet the cat detested him, having gone so far as to take a Nixon in one of his red antique dead man's shoes in the not-so-distant past. The cat walked a few steps into the living room, swished her tail several times rather violently, then turned around, walked back into the bedroom, jumped up on the bed, and went back to sleep.

"Not a bad idea," I said.

Sometime later, as I was working on my third espresso and my first cigar of the day, and deeply involved in the process of feeding the cat a can of Classic Mariner's Entree, I heard a loud ejaculation from somewhere in my living room. I turned to see Ratso standing at my desk holding the Big Chief tablet in his hand.

"Jesus Christ!" he shouted. "Is this a death threat?"

I puffed rather laconically on my cigar a few times and made an attempt to look like a man feeding a cat. This was exactly what I didn't want to happen. For one thing, it was none of Ratso's business. For another, it could prove to be quite a social embarrassment for me if Ratso learned that I'd been writing drunken death threats to the lesbian dance captain in the loft above. Ratso would, no doubt, tell the world, and it would sound crazy to anyone who heard about it. Almost as crazy as wearing candles on your hat.

" 'You've left a hole in my life,' " quoted Ratso from the note. " 'If it's the last thing I do, I'll see that you pay for it.' "

At last, I gave up pretense of calm and rushed over to the desk hastily grabbing the "death note" from Ratso's hands. He appeared somewhat stunned at the intensity of my reactions and I tried belatedly to put him off the trail.

"Just a case I'm working on," I said, making an effort to appear moderately disinterested. I folded the incriminating note and, in what I hoped was a cool, dismissive manner, put it in my pocket.

"Must be some case," said Ratso.

"Let's go to Big Wong's," I said.

Mentioning Chinatown to Ratso was a ploy that almost always worked. The idea of going to a meal anywhere with anyone who was likely to pick up the check almost always worked with Ratso. He was by nature a kindhearted spirit, but when it came time to pay the bill he invariably had fishhooks in his pockets.

Thus it was that in a very short period of time we found ourselves bundled up against the cold, heading down Mott Street toward Big Wong's Restaurant. In very short order we'd been greeted by the friendly waiters in their traditional Eastern fashion: "Ooooh-lah-lah! Oooohh-lah-lah! Kee-Kee! Chee-Chee!"

The precise definition of Kee-Kee and Chee-Chee has been open to quite a bit of good-natured debate in the past. Either they are terms of endearment, or they refer to some aspects of each of our personal identities, or the waiters believe Ratso and I are homosexual lovers, or the two of us have been the butt of a long-running campaign of vicious anti-Occidental, conceivably even anti-Semitic, hatred. All that notwithstanding, Ratso always reports that the roast pork is killer bee. Unfortunately, he pronounces the dish as "roast pawk." The waiters, it should be noted, pronounce the word "pawk" exactly the same way as Ratso. In my experience, this is the only example of East meeting West that has ever produced anything approximating common ground.

"Let me see that threatening note again," said Ratso, as he dug enthusiastically into his favorite dish, roast pawk over scrambled eggs.

"Ratso, this is a very confidential case I'm investigating. It's also possibly a very dangerous one. It's not the kind of case I'd feel comfortable sharing with you. Although I could share some of this sour vegetables, squid, and one-thousand-year-old egg."

"What're you talkin' about, Kinkstah? I've been a part of practically every case you've ever undertaken. C'mon, Sherlock. If I'm not Watson, who is?"

Ratso was not wrong in this assessment. He brought a fierce loyalty and charming naïveté to my investigations, and he'd been my partner and confidant in almost all of them. Of course, so had Rambam. And so had McGovern. And so, more recently, had Stephanie DuPont, who was more attractive and more worldly than Ratso, not to mention that she wouldn't've been caught dead in his ridiculous coonskin cap.

"You do make a very fine Watson, Ratso, it's just that—"

"So show me the fucking note."

There was really no reason not to show Ratso the note except that it was nothing but a tissue of horseshit that I'd written myself in a drunken stupor and I was already feeling mildly embarrassed about it and I didn't need Ratso trying to push me around like a little red apple.

"Look around you, Ratso," I said.

Ratso looked around at the sea of Chinese faces, all of them quite literally bent upon eating dishes that looked a lot better than ours.

"So?" he said.

36

"So I can't show it to you *here*," I said, as a new idea crossed my mind. "It's too public a place. But in a few minutes I'll head down to the dumper in the basement. Wait here exactly three minutes then join me in the dumper and I'll let you see the note. Then we'll stagger our departure from the dumper—"

"You always stagger your departure—"

"—and we'll meet back here at the table."

The plan was agreed upon, and moments later I left the back room of Big Wong's and passed beyond Ratso's field of vision. But instead of taking a left and going downstairs to the dumper, I walked straight out of the place, indicating to the waiters that Ratso was still in the back. This was an unusual development for them as well and I could hear them chuckling to each other and muttering "Kee-Kee" and "Chee-Chee" as I hooked a sharp left and ankled it up Mott Street to Canal. I hailed the first hack I saw and rode it all the way back to Vandam Street with a great spirit of joy rising in my heart.

If my plan worked, it'd be the first time in the modern recorded history of man that Larry "Ratso" Sloman had ever been known to pick up the check.

6

I didn't hear from Ratso all that weekend, so I had to assume that the plan had worked or else he'd died of autoerotic asphyxiation in the dumper at Big Wong's. I wasn't precisely gloating over the success of my little scheme, but it did bring home to me the ease with which a thoughtful general can manipulate his unwitting troops. After all, you're not really using people if you use them for the greater good of man.

"Just as every Jesus needs a Judas," I said to the cat that fateful Sunday night, "every Sherlock needs a Watson. But just *who* that Watson is may be a matter of some argument and conjecture. This can be all for the good, of course, and this fabled 'threat note' may come in quite handy in the course of things."

I showed the cat the threatening note and she appeared to peruse it with extreme studiousness. Then she yawned and went back to sleep.

Alas, a new plan was forming in my mind, a plan much more grandiose and far-reaching than merely tricking Ratso into picking up a check. The way I saw it, the scheme easily could be set into motion and it could be a lot of fun. Any groundbreaking stratagem always has its risks, of course, but these risks I was prepared to take. Indeed, for some years now I'd been prepared to take almost anything.

So it was that, at the tail end of a tedious weekend full of nothing substantial at all, I sat at my desk smoking a cigar and sipping a cup of Kona coffee and realizing that at last I wasn't propping my feet up on the desk. My life had purpose. As they say in Hollywood, I could make a difference. In fact, if the Baby Jesus decided to smile upon my little project, I could make at least two differences. One difference would be to clear up once and for all the murky, deep waters concerning the question of who amongst the small but fervent band of Village Irregulars had the true makings of the perfect Watson. Resolving this matter could be of vital importance in future investigations.

I puffed perhaps a trifle patronizingly upon the cigar and reflected very briefly upon the Watson-like qualities possessed by each of my friends. Ratso, of course, had the loyalty and naïveté areas staked out. But McGovern also was fiercely loyal and possessed with even more childlike innocence than Ratso, which was pretty good for an adult. McGovern brought another quality to the party as well. He was a mensch. A decent human being. This counted heavily, I felt, because it was the true essence of Watson, and decency, of course, was a quality quite foreign to Ratso.

"So, in summation," I said to the cat, who now, quite inexplicably, seemed to be listening intently, "we cannot expect everyone, nor do we wish everyone to be an adult Van Halen fan. If that were the case the world would be a tragic, not to mention rather tedious, place. Of course, it is anyway, but that's not Van Halen's fault. It's Michael Bolton's fault. But, no matter, Ratso and McGovern both have these wonderful, Dr. Watson–like, Peter Pan–Lost Boy–like, maddeningly innocent approaches to life that make you feel like you've swallowed your own vomit."

The cat, of course, said nothing, but she did appear to be studying my forehead with a rather sudden keen gaze.

"Nothing personal, you understand."

I poured a fresh cup of coffee and had just taken it over and set it down on the desk when a small chunk of plaster detached itself from the ceiling and, much to the cat's joy and excitement, fell directly into the cup.

"That's a sign from God," I said to the cat, picking the plaster out of the cup and proceeding to drink the coffee. "Also, it may give me a little buzz."

Actually, though I didn't tell the cat, I did not believe the plaster falling into the coffee was a sign from God. The lesbian dance class had been rehearsing on and off the whole damn weekend and it was not unlikely that still more plaster was going to fall. The fact that it fell into my practically antique Imus in the Morning coffee cup was the work, I believed, of the devil herself, possibly puking her evil onto this planet in the mortal guise of Moriarty just as I was contemplating the essentially gentle conscience of man in the form of Dr. Watson. I took it as a sign, nonetheless, to continue in my glorious quest.

"Rambam and Stephanie are the other two obvious candidates for Watson. They're both highly efficient and wise to the ways of the world. Neither is very innocent and neither lends anything approaching naïveté to any case, though they are both certainly not without charm. Stephanie could pick her nose and still be mesmerizingly charming, though it's doubtful that she's ever picked her nose, belched, farted, pissed, puked, hosed, or taken a Nixon in her life. I've done all those things. Never, of course, at the same time."

The cat wrinkled her nose in an unmistakable gesture of disgust. She twitched her whiskers a bit for good measure and gave forth a highly expressive mew of distaste. This feline behavior hardly surprised me. Cats are neurotically clean and hygienic, just like Stephanie DuPont. When they're not busy sleeping through things, they're busy pretending they never happened. Cats are like women, except that they don't, barring special cases, have sexual relationships with men. Cats, indeed, are very much like lesbians.

Which brought me to the second, and possibly more gratifying aspect of my plan. This was going to be fun. It was getting late, however, seriously past Cinderella time, and I'd hardly gotten any sleep the whole weekend. Some of my state of exhaustion was probably caused by the enormous energy expended in laboriously attempting to explain to the cat the method in my madness. Some of my stress was no doubt induced by the rigors of my work, though at the moment, I had to admit, there did not seem to be a smudge on my docket. But the main reason my eyes currently resembled two piss-holes in the snow could be directly attributable to Winnie Katz and her wonderful lesbian dance class.

For a variety of reasons I hadn't mentioned it to the cat, but very soon, if I didn't miss my guess, Winnie Katz was going to be the one losing sleep. I almost felt sorry for her. As for myself, I fell into a deep and peaceful sleep that night. I dreamed that Joan of Arc was wearing my black cowboy hat. She had candles on the hat and stars in her eyes. And she was dancing.

7

THE building at 199B Vandam where the cat and I lived was an old converted warehouse that had seen better days. There've been times I've felt that I've seen better days myself. Somehow, both of us are still standing. The question of how much a structure can take with Winnie and her girls constantly pounding down on it from the top and Vinnie and Gepetto incessantly banging away from the bottom is anybody's call. I'd already been sandwiched by that ceiling once and I did not relish the prospect of the damn thing collapsing again, this time possibly killing myself, the cat, and, very likely, Vinnie and Gepetto as well.

"Oh, the humanity!" I said to the cat, as we waited at the window for the workmen to arrive.

The cat, of course, said nothing.

A lot of people had been saying nothing for a long time now, I thought, as I plucked a half-smoked Cuban cigar from the Texas-shaped ashtray on the desk. My social intercourse, in fact, even with the Village Irregulars had been decidedly weak lately. All that was about to change, I reflected, as I smiled at the little black puppet head on top of the refrigerator. The puppet head looked me in the eyes and smiled right back. You don't see that kind of simple, genuine, human interaction much in New York these days. The city either needs fewer people or more puppet heads.

The first thing I did after lighting the half-smoked cigar— "They're gamier when resurrected," as Churchill once observed—was to pour a quick espresso down my neck and roust McGovern on the blower.

"Leap sideways!" I shouted, when he finally picked up the phone.

"Unpleasant," said McGovern.

" 'Here hath been dawning another blue day. Think! Wilt thou let it slip useless away?' "

"Unpleasant," said McGovern.

"A lot of things seem unpleasant to us, McGovern, and then later, upon reflection, we realize that they were not merely unpleasant but truly hideous."

"Like trying to answer the phone when you're taking a dump?"

"I sensed the absence of your usual irritating gentile optimism. As a detective, I should've suspected the nature of your current circumstances."

"Now that you know, you'd better make it fast. One look at this apartment should've told you I'm not exactly an anal retentive."

"Call me back when you've completed your Nixon," I said.

It was a measure of McGovern's gentle spirit that the big man could not even become truly aggravated when answering the phone in mid-dump. Nixonius interruptibus is a rather common circumstance in our busy lives today and few if any of us, if we're honest with ourselves, can say that we handle the situation with as much grace and human dignity as McGovern. Of course, that and a quarter will buy you entry to a pay toilet.

By the time Vinnie came in the door and flipped me the puppet head, McGovern still had not called back. At ten-thirty sharp, the lesbian dance class kicked into high gear overhead. About five minutes later, Vinnie and Gepetto, like primitives locked in some pagan ritual, were scraping and pounding on the ceiling with rhythms of their own. It was in this rather tedious time frame that McGovern returned my call.

"Start talkin'," I said, picking up the blower on the left. I maintained two red telephones on my desk, precisely equidistant from where the cat usually sat in the middle. Both phones were connected to the same line, so if the cat was in residence when they rang, she often became highly agitated. I, on the other paw, took the whole situation with a grain of marching powder. I, of course, was not precisely equidistant from the two red ringing blowers.

"I'm done," said McGovern.

"That's a blessing."

"You're telling me. Say, what's all that racket over there? I can hardly hear you."

"Just some lesbians, some Italians, and some garbage trucks."

"You wouldn't think a few lesbians, Italians, and garbage trucks could make all that racket. It sounds almost like New York."

"Add a few Jews, a few sirens—"

"Add a few *million* Jews—"

"Ah, McGovern, the ugly head of anti-Semitism rises again, doesn't it?"

"Better than no head rising at all."

"Look," I said with a bit of irritation, "I really do need to discuss something important with you today. Can we meet for lunch?"

"Sure. I'm drier than a nun's nasty."

"Okay. Gary Cooper time at LaLobotomy?" I said, referring to a little French place that was run by a Greek and that was actually called LaBonBonierre.

"See you there," said McGovern. "Can you give me a little hint as to what this is all about?"

"No," I said, as I cradled the blower.

Especially when all the thuddings and scrapings and bangings were going on, I'd taken to staying away from the living room proper and spending most of my time at my desk, or lurking in the bedroom or the dumper, or pacing back and forth in the narrow corridor of the kitchen. This just seemed like good common sense, though it was rather restricting, particularly since I'd wanted for some time to have a quiet word with Vinnie. Having a quiet word with anybody in the loft these days, unfortunately, was very much akin to whispering on a subway platform. The way the whole place seemed to be vibrating at the moment it could've been a subway platform. I never ride the subway myself. Neither did Willie Mays, so I don't feel too bad about it. Of course, if your place of residence already has the ambience of a subway station you should probably stick to riding in hacks. It's a little more expensive, but you meet a lot of interesting people who come from countries that begin with an "I."

"Vinnie," I said, when he'd come over to the kitchen for an espresso break, "I don't want to ruffle any feathers, but I want to get something straight with you about this espresso machine."

"I'm listenin'," said Vinnie, somewhat guardedly.

"Joe sent this to me after I rescued his daughter from a mugger in a bank ten years ago."

"Good story."

"It's no story. It's the truth."

"Look," said Vinnie. "I'm gonna tell you something and you keep it to yourself because dis thing smells fishy and after doin' all dis work on your ceiling I wouldn't want to find out you ended up visiting the fish."

"That wouldn't really be very cost-effective, would it?"

"Not really," said Vinnie, with a smile that never reached his eyes. "You sure dis happened ten years ago?"

"I'm positive. Why?"

"Because dese numbers ain't crunchin' right and in dis business somebody's head could get crunched instead. You see, Joe *did* have a daughter, but we got a little problem here."

"What is our little problem?"

"She died three years before you saved her in the bank."

8

LaLOBOTOMY, or LaBonBonierre as most people called it, may have had a French name but was actually one of the best greasy spoons in the Village. Charles, the Greek who ran the place and cooked as well, was possessed of a friendly spirit and a dedication to his work that is quite rare today in New York or even in America. Although McGovern lived on Jane Street, merely half a block from LaLobotomy, he was nonetheless late for our little lunch affair. It wasn't the power-lateness of a busy executive, however. It was more in the style of the fashionable lateness of Marilyn Monroe. Marilyn and McGovern had more in common than simply being late. They both had realized that all great love is hopeless. She always kept a picture of Abe Lincoln, whom she adored, on her bedside table. McGovern didn't have any room on his bedside table or on any other level surface in his apartment, but he did keep a photo of Carole Lombard, whom he adored, on his wall next to the fireplace. McGovern and Marilyn belong to that special group of humans who secretly believe they are knights and ladies born out of their time, and they may well be right. They are incurable dreamers with impeccable taste and they know that the dead invariably make cheap dates. They are spiritual necrophiliacs who have never and will never consummate their relationships. It's better to love the dead, I figured, as Charles came over with the coffee, than it is to kill the dream. The tables at LaLobotomy suddenly looked like the ones Van Gogh had painted in *Night Cafe*. Marilyn, Abe, and Carole, no doubt, had already left the place. McGovern, of course, hadn't gotten here yet. Charles tilted the pot deftly backward with his left hand as he poured the coffee into my cup.

"Nice backhand," I said.

Moments later, McGovern came into the place, waved Charles a friendly greeting, and sat down across from me at the little table. He was a large man with a large, handsome head, and a large laugh that was often quite a bit too loud for indoor use. He'd personally interviewed many mass murderers including Richard Speck, Lt. Rusty Calley, and Charles Manson. He'd also, for several years, been in charge of the society page for the *Daily News*. I'd once asked him which job he found the hardest and he'd told me: "The society page is the real killer."

"You're probably wondering, my dear Watson," I said, "exactly why I wanted to meet you here."

"Charles," said McGovern, "are you still serving breakfast?"

"For you," said Charles, "of course."

"I'll have two eggs looking at me," said McGovern, "along with a tall stack of pancakes, large orange juice, and coffee. Oh, yes, and a side order of ham."

"The ugly head of anti-Semitism," I said.

"Aren't you eating, Kink?"

"No, McGovern. I'm fasting until there's peace and freedom in the world."

"In that case," said McGovern, "make it a double order of ham."

The small insides of LaLobotomy filled up briefly with Mc-

Govern's loud, lilting, Irish laughter, and several patrons stared momentarily at the large man with the large head. Then I ordered. Then we got down to business.

"I'm working on a new case," I said, with an air of intrigue. "I haven't spoken to anyone else about this and I'm probably not going to. You'll soon see why I'm playing it so close to the vest."

"With a vest like yours," said McGovern, "I can understand the problem."

McGovern was making reference to the rather disreputable-looking, but highly efficient no-hunting vest I often wore in colder weather. In the loops stitched across it, instead of shotgun shells, were half a dozen half-smoked cigars.

"At any rate, McGovern, I never told you this, but I believe you may have within your being the very essence of the perfect Watson. You're the only one of the Village Irregulars I know I can trust where a life might be at stake. I need you now, Watson."

"I can't do it," said McGovern. "I have a dentist appointment in two hours."

"What's more important? Somebody's teeth or the truth?"

"That depends," laughed McGovern. "Whose teeth? Whose truth? Anyway, I thought Ratso was your choice for Dr. Watson."

As Charles brought the food and poured more coffee, I realized that the situation needed to be handled very carefully. If McGovern got into some kind of snit it could last for days and fairly well torpedo my little plan. I spoke fondly but lightly of Ratso.

"Ratso is Ratso," I said. "He'll never change his wardrobe, his careless, brash, New York persona, or his total inability to recognize, much less understand, the criminal mind. He has over ten thousand books on Hitler, Jesus, and Bob Dylan. If I ever get a case involving Hitler, Jesus, and Bob Dylan, he'd make a brilliant one-man dream team. For anything else, I'm afraid he's just a colorful old friend. You, McGovern, are the one who may just be worthy of the name Watson."

I was laying it on pretty thick and McGovern seemed to be taking it all in rather soberly, which was saying a lot for McGovern, who could pour vodka down his neck with the best of them. He was the only living soul I knew who'd actually had a drink named after him. Whether he was humoring me or he was buying it, I couldn't tell for certain. It was time to bring out the artillery.

"What do you make of this?" I said, rather dramatically extracting my drunken note to Winnie from the inside pocket of my vest.

McGovern took the note and started to read and I felt a pang of guilt as I noticed, not for the first time, what a truly trusting spirit he was. When he'd finished reading, his eyes were as wide and awestruck as those of a child.

"Jesus, Mary, and Joseph!" said McGovern.

"Dysfunctional family if I ever saw one."

"Is it for real?"

"My client thinks so."

"Who's your client?"

"Winnie Katz."

My initial wavelet of guilt about deceiving McGovern had dissipated almost totally upon the beach of no regrets. None of the Village Irregulars had even returned my phone calls over the weekend. They had their lives, and when it suited them, they'd help me. All the times I'd been drowning in loneliness they were never there. Now I was going to have some fun and maybe give Winnie back a little bit of the irritation she'd been causing me for years. The whole thing was easy and relatively painless as well as interesting to anyone who's ever dreamed of holding a Watson audition and seeing if anybody came, and I don't mean sexually.

"You can see why it'd be difficult for someone like me to try to invade her Isle of Lesbos in order to investigate. But someone like you, Watson, if I may call you that, has all the power of the Fourth Estate. You could say you're doing an in-depth profile on Winnie and her modern terpsichorean techniques."

"Piece of cake," said McGovern with growing enthusiasm for the project.

"But you're undercover, you see. No direct questions about the note, or the investigation, or my involvement. Winnie's deeply traumatized about the note and whoever or whatever's behind it. Your job is to insinuate yourself into her milieu without imparting any knowledge of the case or your special relationship with me. If she knows your real purpose up there, she may just shut down and then we won't get anything."

"Insinuate myself into her milieu," said McGovern rather suggestively.

"These are *lesbians,* McGovern."

"Well, there's nothing wrong with *looking* at their milieu, is there?"

"Not a thing," I said, smiling to myself at the thought of McGovern ransacking Winnie's liquor cabinet and ogling her young protégées.

"I'm your man, Sherlock," he said, with a dreamy look in his eyes.

"One more thing," I said. "This profile may take some time—"

"Don't worry. I think I'm going to like the work."

"I was going to suggest that before you're through you recruit Mick Brennan to take some photographs of all the principals—"

"Brennan?" said McGovern. "You can't be serious about sending Brennan up there. He could fuck up a—"

"Lesbian dance class? I've thought of that. But we need good, clear photos of everybody up there. No one can be excluded from suspicion. These are deep waters, Watson."

"You're right. I'll sort of test the deep waters for a while, then I'll bring in Brennan. Whatever sicko is behind this death threat, we'll find him."

"Or her," I said.

"Of course."

"And remember, everything we've spoken about is completely confidential. Make a regular pest of yourself if you have to, but don't reveal the fact that you're an integral part of this investigation. It could be hazardous to your health and I don't want to lose the most trustworthy Watson I've ever known. When do you want to start?"

"No time like the present."

"What about your dentist's appointment?"

"What dentist's appointment?"

9

As I walked home through the cold, gray afternoon Village streets, my spirits seemed to be lifting with every step. There was the Tom Sawyer element in all this, I supposed. Getting other people to do the work of irritating people who were irritating you. And, like Tom Sawyer, I didn't see anything wrong with motivating McGovern and the other Village Irregulars into action on my behalf. Indeed, they were very likely getting rather rusty in the Watson department. With the possible exception of Rambam procuring for me the help of Vinnie and Gepetto, it'd been a damn long time since any of them had done anything to help out the Kinkster. And it wasn't like I was sending them into the Valley of Death, I reflected, as I sheltered and lit a half-smoked cigar from my no-hunting vest. I liked my no-hunting vest and disliked hunters more with each passing season. I had now reached the stage in my own spiritual evolution where I celebrated hunting accidents as a sure sign that God, Buddha, Allah, or L. Ron Hubbard was watching over us all.

I wasn't opposed, of course, to hunting for a potential killer, or hunting for the "sicko" who wrote the death threat to Winnie

Katz. Happy hunting, I thought. If McGovern only knew that the culprit was currently walking up Vandam Street, puffing on a half-smoked Cuban cigar, and smiling very much in the fashion of your normal serial killer! On the other paw, how much guilt can you really feel in sending your trusty troops on a little mission to invade a lesbian dance class? What was wrong with a little vicarious escapade like this to break the ennui of another winter in the city? What harm could it do? And also, I thought, as I stepped into the freight elevator in the lobby with the one exposed lightbulb, what red-blooded American male wouldn't want to tackle this assignment? It was a supreme irony these days, I figured, that heterosexual men in this country seemed more interested in lesbians than they did in normal women, if indeed, such creatures as heterosexual men and normal women still roamed the land.

When I walked into the loft the phones were ringing, the lesbians were thudding on the ceiling, and the cat, Vinnie, and Gepetto were nowhere to be seen. On about the fifth ring I collared the blower on the left.

"Start talkin'," I said.

"Kinkstah!" said an unmistakable rodentlike voice. "I was up at Woodstock yesterday so I didn't get to return your message. What's happenin', Kinkstah?"

"Rats, this is important. Can you meet me at the Monkey's Paw around five o'clock this afternoon? It's about the threat note."

"You mean the threat note that you didn't leave in the dumper at Big Wong's?"

"It was just too risky, Ratso. I thought better of it. I hope you didn't have a problem with the check."

"Don't worry," said Ratso, chuckling to himself. "I took care of it. I got 'em to run a tab for you."

"One should never underestimate your ingenuity, Watson. So you'll meet me at the Paw at five?"

"I'll be the guy wearing the coonskin cap, the green cowboy boots, and the red batik Ubangi caftan."

"Quite the clotheshorse," I said.

After a while, the cat seemed to materialize from nowhere. A short time later, Vinnie and Gepetto returned from an extended lunch break. Soon after that, I retired into the bedroom for a little power nap. Before I knew it, it was time to meet Ratso at the Monkey's Paw. When you have a lot of things going on in your life, time seems to have a funny little habit of goose-stepping right by you.

"And time," I said to the cat, as I grabbed a few cigars for the road, "is the money of love. Too bad we're broke."

The workmen had gone for the day, leaving little if any sign of progress. The cat was curled up under her own private heat lamp on my desk. With one eye half open, she watched me put on my coat and hat and start for the door.

"You're in charge," I said.

Perhaps she was. Perhaps that's why the lesbian dance class, which had been silent since I'd awakened from my power nap, now started up again, almost like a Greek tragic chorus not content to let me have my own exit line. Perhaps the pounding on the ceiling was not the work of mortals at all. Perhaps it was a great, natural, eternal phenomenon like the winds or the tides. Perhaps, as with Don Quixote, it was a giant windmill that I could only conquer perhaps by losing or gaining my own sanity. But would it still be there if no one was in the loft to hear it? That was why I left the cat in charge, I thought. I closed the door and, I suppose, the cat closed her eye.

My cookie-duster had barely made contact with my pint of Guinness, which had a better head on it than most people I know, when I felt a heavy hand on my shoulder and heard a loud, grating voice beating a familiar tattoo on my left ear drum.

"Kinkstah!" said Ratso. "What ya drinkin', Kinkstah?"

"Guinness," I said. "The drink that kept the Irish from taking over the world. It's a good thing, too, because what the hell would you do with it once you took it over?"

"I'd fuck Christianne Amanpour and I'd play hockey at the Sky Rink anytime I wanted instead of having to play at two o'-clock in the morning."

"While not especially lofty, these are legitimate aims and ideals of yours, Ratso. I wonder what kind of drink it would take to keep the Jews from taking over the world?"

"That's easy," said Ratso, pulling up a barstool next to me. "Evian water."

Ratso made a point of ordering the most expensive wine in the place and swirling it around in his glass until he just about drove me crazy. Fortunately, the most expensive wine in the Monkey's Paw is not all that expensive.

"I hope that's not French wine," I said. "I'm currently boy-cotting all French products."

"Why?"

"Because they hang geese upside down and they nuked about half the South Pacific several years ago just out of pride and arrogance."

"But they did take in Baby Doc Duvalier," said Ratso.

"There's only one Frenchman I truly admire. Two, if you want to count Joan of Arc."

"Forget her," said Ratso.

"Then there's only one Frenchman I truly admire. He's the greatest Frenchman of them all."

"Seeing as you're a detective," said Ratso, "I'll skip over Voltaire, Victor Hugo, and Gauguin, and go right to Inspector Maigret. Am I right, Sherlock?"

"Close, Watson, very close. But as we all know, Inspector Mai-gret was merely a fictional creation of Simenon. Simenon was one of my three favorite Belgians, other than waffle, of course. The other two are Father Damien and Hercule Poirot, who also is a fictional character of Agatha Christie's. It's just possible that all of us are fictional characters in some perverse comedy that never did much box office. Maybe that's why we spend our lives searching for meaning that just isn't there, or for truth that we wouldn't recognize if it was."

"How about another Guinness for the Kinkster!" Ratso shouted to the bartender. "And I'll have another glass of this excellent wine. Is it French?"

"Does the Pope shit in the woods?" said the bartender brusquely.

"Guess it's not French," I said.

"Pity," said Ratso. "It has such a delicate bouquet. Now what about the goddamn threat note?"

"Ah, Watson, nothing escapes you."

Because Ratso's catlike curiosity had already been quite piqued by the note, and because he'd very possibly believed he was Dr. Watson for over ten years now, it was an easy matter to procure his involvement in my little adventure. The two of us proceeded to pore over the note together furtively at the bar, even as the bartender poured us both another round.

"Whoever wrote this means business," said Ratso. "He's got to be one sick fuck."

"Let's not jump to conclusions, Ratso. It could be a woman who wrote this note. Possibly a former lover of Winnie's."

"Possibly a former lover of mine," said Ratso. "Over the years I've had a few broads go gay on me."

"Hard to believe," I said.

I gave Ratso pretty much the same spiritual pep talk I'd given McGovern earlier in the day. He was the perfect Dr. Watson. He was the only one of the Village Irregulars I could really count on when a life might very easily be hanging in the balance. He was the one with the interpersonal skill, brains, ingenuity, and sensitivity, not to mention perseverance, required to truly determine the lay of the land in Winnie's mysterious, exclusive domain.

"I like that 'lay of the land,' " said Ratso. "Give me a day or two. I'll figure out a surefire way to crash Winnie's party without tipping our hand. That's one thing Howard Stern and I have in common, you know. When I ghosted both of his books I got to know him pretty well and he's obsessed with lesbians. I'll tell you a little secret. I am, too. Lesbians really turn me on."

I was almost feeling sorry for Winnie Katz again. Almost. Ratso, I knew from past experience, was ruthlessly relentless about getting into scenes and places in which he wasn't wanted. Indeed, that may have been his long suit. I was counting on him to play it successfully again.

"Remember," I said, "say nothing to Winnie, or to anyone else for that matter, about the investigation or the death threat, but gather all the information you can about her and her girls. Winnie knows me, so I can't very well spy on her myself. The job may call for a deep, dedicated mole."

"I can do it, Sherlock. I may even be able to tape some things that Howard could use later on his radio show."

"Very possibly, Watson, very possibly."

"Now tell me," said Ratso, "who's the greatest Frenchman of them all?"

"Why, Le Petomane, of course. The guy who had a farting act at the Moulin Rouge from 1892 to 1914. He could emit sounds both tenderly and aggressively, like a cannon or an opera singer, or a well-played trombone, and he could actually fart melodies. Le Petomane regularly outdrew even great stars like Sarah Bernhardt, and many luminaries including the King of Belgium came to see his act. At the end of every show he'd always blow a candle out with his ass. His real name was Joseph Pujol, and he died in 1945 at the age of eighty-eight."

"I wonder if I could find some books on Le Petomane?"

"You could then become the world's leading authority on Hitler, Jesus, Bob Dylan, and Le Petomane."

"Great idea, Sherlock. I'll do some research. In the meantime, I'd like to offer a little toast to Le Petomane."

Ratso tilted toward me on the barstool until his coonskin cap nearly touched my shoulder. He then proceeded to blast an almost eerie, long-lasting soprano fart which, I must say, caught several nearby couples somewhat off their guard. Ratso, of course, was totally oblivious to the various expressions of horror and distaste.

"Do you think he might've sounded something like that?" he asked, finally sitting upright on the barstool.

"Close, Watson," I said. "Very close."

IO

T HE pieces were rapidly falling into place, I thought, as I
waited for Rambam on Tuesday morning in a dim-sum restaurant in Chinatown. The place was as large and as crowded as
Grand Central Station, and when the girls pushing carts of
chicken feet came by and shouted in your ear, it was almost as
loud. McGovern and Ratso, of course, had been child's play
compared to the challenge that Rambam might present. Rambam was a licensed private investigator who'd spent time inside
federal never-never land and he certainly hadn't just fallen off
the turnip truck where criminal behavior was concerned. While
Ratso and McGovern basically believed in the essential good-
ness of people, Rambam, I felt, saw human nature more accu-
rately for what it was: Le Petomane farting out the candles on
Van Gogh's hat.

I was sitting at a big round table with what appeared to be an
extended Chinese family, including grandparents and adorable
small children who looked like mischievous little tadpoles. Little Asian children never bothered the Kinkster. Blond, Aryan
Little Lord Fauntleroys, however, never failed to get up my

sleeve. Maybe it was my years of Peace Corps experience in the Far East, but it seemed as if these small, bright-eyed Chinese kids were the sons and daughters I would never have. Or maybe I did have sons and daughters and they were running around Southeast Asia somewhere. It was hard to know, and I wasn't sure I wanted to.

"Ever seen a real cowboy before?" I asked the kids.

Evidently they hadn't, because they hid their faces in their hands and started giggling. Possibly they muttered *"ang-mo"* to their parents. *"Ang-mo,"* of course, means "red-haired devil."

The family appeared to speak little if any English, so we just smiled and nodded at each other and I ordered some *shu mai* and a big bowl of black snails that everybody in the place seemed to be sucking up. Seven hundred Chinese can't be totally out where the buses don't run. I found myself wishing that Rambam would hurry up, however, so I wouldn't be the only red-haired devil in the whole damn restaurant.

When I finally saw Rambam's clean-cut, well-muscled, familiar form threading its way through the crowded room I felt a small twinge of doubt about the mission upon which I would soon try to send him. After all, I did not like to deliberately mislead Rambam; he'd saved my life on several occasions, not the least of which was giving me the Heimlich Maneuver at a Sunday hotel brunch in Kerrville, Texas, where an old man kept playing the piano and good little Christian church workers and their families pretended nothing was happening as five feet away a man was choking to death. Unfortunately, the man was me. I'd been reading the *Houston Chronicle* while eating a prime rib. Flipping the pages, I saw a small head of Kirk Douglas, a small head of the football player The Boz, and then suddenly a big head of myself. This, as you can imagine, gave me rather a big head myself, and I quickly swallowed a large piece of prime rib in my excitement to show the pic to Rambam.

As I looked admiringly at the big head of Kinky I could feel the meat lodge firmly in my throat in such a way that I couldn't speak, or gurgle, or even make the usual choking sounds. When you can't make choking sounds it's a pretty good bet you're choking to death. My first thought, of course, was of Mama Cass. My second was that choking to death because you got so excited when you looked in a newspaper and saw that your own head was bigger than Kirk Douglas's or Brian Bosworth's could trap you in your vanity forever and become the thing you were forever known for, as it had, undoubtedly, with Mama Cass eating a ham sandwich, or Nelson Rockefeller hosing his secretary. People rarely give a damn who you are or what kind of a life you've lived, but if you choke to death celebrating the fact that a photo of your head is bigger than Kirk Douglas's or Brian Bosworth's, that's the kind of news folks can get their teeth into. Fortunately, Rambam had had EMS training and was able to execute a successful Heimlich Maneuver that rapidly propelled a large chunk of half-eaten prime rib twenty feet across the room onto a table of a good, well-dressed, churchgoing couple and several blond Aryan children, all of whom had so zealously ignored their neighbor's near-death experience that they thought the mysterious object was a meteorite.

How could I, in good faith, attempt to suck, fuck, or cajole Rambam's involvement in my merry little prank? Quite easily, it would seem. For one thing, the wheels were already in motion and I doubted if even the Pentagon had the power or the wherewithal at this late date in the operation to stop McGovern and Ratso from attempting to breach Winnie's walls. Also, the very thought of the Village Irregulars, a gang that couldn't shoot straight if there ever was one, a collection of eccentric individuals totally unknown to Winnie Katz, running rampant indefinitely through her precious, private, pristine lesbian paradise was almost funny enough to make me choke on my chicken feet. It was a good thing Rambam had finally arrived at the table.

"Have some chicken feet," I said. "They're probably one of the reasons my triglycerides are over four hundred."

"When they get to five hundred," said Rambam, "sell."

Rambam nodded and smiled at all three generations of the Chinese family and they nodded and smiled back. My plan with Rambam was to get him to place an electronic eavesdropping device somewhere in Winnie's studio so we could monitor everything that went on up there. Though illegal, of course, it seemed to me to pretty much fall into the category of harmless fun. Not only would I be able to follow the foibles and pandemonium engendered by the infiltration of the Village Irregulars, but I also might finally discover what the hell was really going on up there. As a red-blooded American heterosexual, I'd often suspected that much of the action might be other than dance-related.

"First of all," said Rambam, once I'd explained what I wanted from him, "have you interviewed the victim?"

"Of course," I said. "But Winnie was very stressed about the threat note and the whole situation and she doesn't want people to know about this. You're people."

"I understand," said Rambam. "If Winnie were my client I'd insist upon interviewing her, as any decent PI would. But since you're my client and my friend, I'll take your word for it."

"My word is my bond," I said, "though I understand the bond market's not doing too well."

"Did you ask Winnie whom she suspects?"

"She's very paranoid. She suspects everyone."

"That's a start. Did you ask her about jilted heterosexual lovers? Jilted gay lovers? Professional rivals? Landlords? Business partners?"

"She has no idea," I said. "She's very sensitive about all this, as you can understand. About all we have to go on is sort of a premonition of hers that her life may be in danger—and this note which she gave me."

As Rambam studied the note I reflected lightly on the fact that the more you tell a lie the easier it gets to tell it. But there was no dangerous perpetrator lurking in the shadows here. The only perpetrator was me and the only thing I was perpetrating was a harmless little prank upon someone who'd not only disrupted my sleep pattern for years but who now seemed to take no responsibility whatever for the damage she'd done to my ceiling and my person. A little payback was certainly in order, I thought.

"Graphology," said Rambam, still perusing the note, "is the art of analyzing handwriting. It's a fairly inexact science, but lately I've come across a really skilled graphologist. I'd like to show him this note and see what he comes up with."

"Is that really necessary?" I said, reaching for the paper, which Rambam did not release from his grasp. "I mean the intent behind this letter is obvious."

"You might be surprised," continued Rambam, "at what the graphologist may be able to tell us about the person who wrote this note."

"I'm sure," I said, "but I need to keep this copy. It's the only concrete evidence we have. I may need to show it to the police."

"Okay," said Rambam, "so make me a copy."

"I make copy now," said the Chinese waiter, who'd been standing behind us for the past five minutes. "Have Xerox machine in back."

"There you go," said Rambam, handing the note to the waiter and watching him scuttle away toward the back of the restaurant. "You didn't tell me you were bringing Charlie Chan into the investigation."

"At the moment I just want to know if Steve Rambam can find an effective way to bug Winnie Katz's loft."

"No problem," said Rambam. "I could be the guy from Con Ed inspecting the gas meter."

"It worked before," I said. "That's how you got us into the Nazi's place on the Upper East Side several years back."

"If it worked with a Nazi," said Rambam, "it'll work with a lesbian."

"There's a certain twisted logic to that," I admitted. "So when the bug's in place I'll be able to hear everything that's going on up there?"

"I'll put the receiver right in the middle of your fucking desk between your two red telephones. You can turn it on any time you want and hear 'The Lesbian Hour of Power.' "

"Great," I said. "When can you do it?"

"I could probably have it in, if all goes well, by sometime this weekend."

"Hell, this is Monday. What takes so long?"

"What takes so long is that I'm trying to wrap up several other cases. Cases, I might add, in which people are paying me for my work. One of them's just about nailed though. A guy who burned down his own warehouse for the insurance money. In the trade, it's called Jewish lightning."

"Jewish lightning?" I said. "I thought that was a joke."

"It's no joke," said Rambam. "I've handled literally dozens of these cases. And the funny thing about Jewish lightning is it seems to strike over and over again in exactly the same place. It's a far-off, magic, fairy-tale kingdom where most people like yourself have probably never even set foot."

"What's the name of the place?"

"We call it Brooklyn," said Rambam.

II

I did not feel especially comfortable with Rambam's having a Xeroxed copy of my drunken threat note, but there was nothing I could do about it. When you hire a private investigator, there's always the chance that he might actually try to investigate. Graphology, as Rambam had said, was a very inexact science. I wasn't too worried about anything personally incriminating coming out of the note. If it worked for Patsy Ramsey, I figured, it ought to work for the Kinkster. The only thing I'd forgotten to discuss with Rambam, in fact, was a small matter that had totally slipped my mind when Charlie Chan had suddenly offered to Xerox the note. It was the little point of curiosity as to whether Joe the Hyena's daughter had stepped on a rainbow within the past ten years or thirteen years ago, which, of course, would've made her ineligible for me to rescue at any bank except the Jonah & Job Branch of the First Spiritual Savings and Loan. Whatever the reason for the discrepancy, it was a matter, I figured, that would keep. At the moment, I had bigger fish to fry and the next one I hoped to hook was very likely going to be hell to reel in.

Stephanie DuPont had not been in contact with me since the week before when the ceiling had collapsed on my head. She'd found me lying in a pool of plaster in the middle of the living room and she'd run upstairs to bring me some brandy. But once she discovered I was basically ambulatory and unhurt except for a slightly damaged ego, she proceeded almost immediately to blip off the screen. That's about all you could expect from home care these days, I figured.

With Rambam, Ratso, McGovern, and Brennan all solidly under my belt, Sherlock had never had it so good. Now, if I could reach Stephanie's fiercely feminist consciousness with a hint at the horrible homophobic heterosexual plot against poor little lesbian Winnie, she might just jump on the boat as well.

"His Kinkyship sails at dawn!" I shouted to anyone who was listening that afternoon.

Unfortunately, Vinnie, Gepetto, and the cat all happened to be listening, thanks in large part to a momentary respite from the lesbian dance class. By this time the two Italian workmen, being in total ignorance of my behind-the-scenes master plan, had come to regard me, not unkindly, as a rather benign eccentric who was undoubtedly cookin' on another planet. The cat, needless to say, had known this for years. This was, of course, precisely what I wanted them to think.

"Hi, darling," I said, moments later when I got Stephanie on the phone.

"Hello, dickhead," she said.

"Thanks for discovering my body last week. If you hadn't come along when you did, the cat probably would've eaten me."

"She's about the only female in the world who would've."

"I wouldn't be so sure, my chaste Aryan goddess."

"I'm sure, my lecherous Jewish Chia-pet."

"Okay," I said, "so how about we have dinner tonight?"

"How about I put your dick in the Cuisinart?"

Stephanie DuPont, for one so young, was well on her merry

67

way to becoming the biggest ball-buster of all time. But she was funny. She was brilliant. And she was beautiful beyond a shipwrecked sailor's dream. Beneath her icy exterior, where few if any prospectors had survived the caustic blizzard of her nature, there beat a heart of gold. I was crazy, perverse, misguided, romantic, egocentric, stupid, and smart enough to believe that if I followed my map I could reach the mother lode.

"Eight o'clock?" I said. "The Derby?"

"I'll see you there, dickhead," said Stephanie. "Unlike you, I've got some work to do."

I had to admit that Vinnie and Gepetto were making progress. Of course, I was making progress, too. If things went well with Stephanie tonight, I'd have four operatives in place by the time Rambam had the transmitter installed over the weekend. Then I could sit back and, yes, put my feet up on the desk, and listen as Winnie received the full brunt of the Kinky experience. I couldn't wait for McGovern to accidentally break Winnie's favorite piece of furniture. Or Brennan, the self-proclaimed "failed boy toy," to deeply offend one of Winnie's girls and get into an ugly, crude, prolonged, yet possibly very witty, shouting match. Or Ratso, dressed preposterously, trying to eat everything and everyone in the house and then, if the gods were with us, demonstrating his quite remarkable farting abilities. And I could just see Winnie and every single one of her protégées absolutely and quite futilely salivating over Stephanie DuPont.

"All in all," I said to the cat, "it certainly promises to be a week that Winnie will never forget."

The cat, of course, said nothing. She simply raised her head rather smugly and stared at the ceiling. Moments later, the lesbian dance class started up again.

There's a special way to talk to a beautiful woman, and if you don't know the way, you can be in for an awkward and rather painful experience. You've got to show her that, while you're aware of her obvious beauty, there are other aspects of life that have fascinated you so completely that they've made you the kind of person that you are. You do not live because of her beauty, but yet, you're able to appreciate it. You live to become the first man to circumnavigate Lake Stupid, or to get a government grant to sculpt a skyscraper-sized scrotum, or to shoot and kill one of every kind of animal in the world and stuff their heads with your dreams, or to become a stand-up tragedy, or to write the great Armenian novel, or to wander off into the wilderness or the suburbs until you cease to exist or have to get dressed up to take out the trash, which is pretty much the same thing, or to bake Amish friendship bread or to win many wars and football games for Jesus. *That's* what you live for, and if she's lucky, she might someday get to be a *part* of it. The point is to always let her know you have other interests besides her.

"Have you ever heard of Le Petomane?" I said, as we sat across from each other at a cozy little table.

"No," said Stephanie, "but I'm sure you're pronouncing it wrong."

"I hardly think so," I said. "I'm quite sure of the pronunciation. I just don't know the meaning."

"And you never will. So who was Le Petomane?"

"He was the French farting champion at the turn of the century."

"Lordy!" said Stephanie. "I shaved my legs for this?"

"I shaved my back for it."

"Friedman, don't you have anything better to do than make up crude stories to repel young girls?"

"Ah, Virginia, you cynical little girl. I didn't make up Le Petomane. There really was such a man. He could make the sounds of instruments and even play recognizable melodies with his ass. He died in 1945, the year after I was born. I'm just sorry I never got to see one of his great performances at the Moulin Rouge."

"Apparently, he passed his gifts along to you."

"They say he could suck in over a gallon of water with his anus and expel it in a violent stream up to distances of more than ten yards."

"Friedman! I'm warning you—"

"Good evening, madam," said the waiter. "And now what would you like to drink?"

We were halfway through the rabbit food and waiting for the big, hairy steaks to arrive when Stephanie announced she planned to attend law school in the fall. Since most of us appear to be drawn to occupations we're hideously ill-suited for, it was mildly heartening to see a ball-buster like her decide to be a lawyer. In fact, it was perfect.

"Great," I said. "Then you'll be really equipped to help me with my investigations. Rambam says the main difference between a private investigator and a lawyer is that a lawyer calls his investigations 'cases' and a private investigator calls his cases 'investigations.' And, of course, the lawyer makes a hell of a lot more money."

"I'm not getting into law for the money," said Stephanie. "I'm going to be an advocate for women's causes."

I almost choked on my baby iceberg lettuce but I recovered quickly. It seemed like I'd been truly blessed. This was not merely perfect. This was fucking kismet.

"Then maybe you ought to take a look at this," I said, once again dragging out the same old deranged, disparaging document that John Jameson and Son had so recently written to Winnie Katz.

"You realize, dickhead," said Stephanie, after devouring the missive like it was the main course, "that this is the work of a true psychopath."

"Let's not rush to judgment," I said, slightly taken aback by the intensity and the uniformity of reaction to the note. "Winnie brought it to me and she's obviously very distressed by it, but it could turn out to be nothing more than a harmless prank."

"Harmless prank, my sweet ass. This should be taken right to the police."

"Winnie doesn't want that," I said quickly. "She wants this handled with the utmost discretion. Which makes me think she might suspect more about this than she's currently telling me."

"Maybe she feels uncomfortable talking to a 'breeder' like yourself. God knows I do."

" 'Breeder,' " I said. "Good to know you're up to date on all the current gay buzz words. I do admit to trying to be a breeder. Haven't had a lot of luck yet—"

"Keep telling your Le Petomane stories and you never will."

"I'm doing what I can to understand and empathize with the lesbian ethos," I said. "I checked my dick and balls at the door."

"Too bad you didn't check your tongue."

"The rack was full."

"And you should've checked that cornball hat."

"That's the only thing Jews and cowboys have in common. They both like to wear their hats indoors."

"You're probably about the only circumcised cowboy in the world."

"That's right. And I sent the circumcision to Fidel Castro so he could plant it and grow little dictators."

"That's not even vaguely amusing. So what're you planning to do to help Winnie?"

"I don't know," I said, feigning weariness and frustration. "Lesbians distrust men so much I don't know where to start. I can't get into Winnie's world enough to even round up the usual suspects."

"Maybe I could!" said Stephanie excitedly, her blue eyes already dancing. "Winnie's been trying to get me to join her dance class for years now."

"You mean you'd boldly go where no man has ever gone before? It could be dangerous."

"Ha!" said Stephanie. "Dangerous? Why do you men always have to be such wimps?"

"Because we can't keep up the payments on our 1957 plastic inflatable testicles. So you're going to join the class?"

"I'll sign up tomorrow. This could be fun. Of course, I'll report in regularly, Sherlock."

"Very good, Watson. Or should I say Irene Adler?"

"Wasn't she the spy who supposedly broke Sherlock's heart?"

"You've already done that once. This is a small company, but we're very gender-friendly. Why don't you be Watson? Go for that old glass ceiling!"

"Only if it falls on your head," she said.

Moments later, over two big, hairy steaks and a bottle of Château de Catpiss, I felt the final piece, so to speak, had fallen firmly into place. I cautioned Stephanie about mentioning the threat note or the investigation to Winnie or any of the girls. I also suggested letting them all warm up to her a bit at least until they reached the point of confiding in her.

"In such fashion, Watson, we may finally learn the dark secrets of the sisters of Sappho."

"That's fine," said Stephanie, "but just remember what my father once told me about dealing with strange circumstances like this."

"What did he say? I always look up to my elders for wisdom and advice."

"Unfortunately, he's not one of your elders. You're older than he is, dickhead."

"That *is* unfortunate. But I still look up to him for wisdom and advice. You *are* his daughter, right?"

"That's *right*, fuckbrain. And don't forget it."

"Fine. Now what worldly wisdom did your old man have to impart?"

"Something that has stood me in good stead ever since I was a small child—"

"You're still a small child—"

"My daddy took me on his knee—"

"Another dysfunctional family."

"—and he said, 'Honey, wherever you go and whatever you do—'"

"Please get to the meat of it."

"'Always remember this—'"

"I'm begging you."

"'Never order a margarita in a Chinese restaurant.'"

12

V ERY few people, indeed, realized what a fiercely private person Winnie was. Not only was there no trace of mankind anywhere in her loft or in her life, but usually she did not even suffer strange straight women very gladly. The thought of such an obstreperous, not to say obnoxious, crew as the Village Irregulars running roughshod for an interminable amount of time through her pristine pastures was almost enough to make me stamp the ledger "paid in full."

You may be wondering how I, a red-blooded American heterosexual, have any knowledge, carnal or otherwise, about Winnie's private life. The answer is really quite simple. Some years back, in another lifetime, as they say, Winnie wavered ever so slightly and I attempted to do what any red-blooded American heterosexual would've done in my position which, sexually speaking, was not missionary. I tried to wean Winnie from her wicked, womanizing ways. Obviously, I was not entirely successful.

Since that long ago time, or very possibly because of it, relations between Winnie and myself had become increasingly strained until the time of this writing in which the strain has become not dissimilar to that of a giant sphincter struggling somewhere amongst the stars to dump upon the earth the accumulated detritus of God. In recent years, I'd visited Winnie's lair on exactly three occasions, twice to drop off the cat, a practice that Winnie has since discouraged, and once, to have a brief conversation at a time when I very definitively needed a checkup from the neck up. It had not been a pleasant conversation. Nor had it been in any way conducive to improving my rapidly deteriorating state of mental hygiene. Thus it was that Winnie Katz and I remained moderately embittered, rather unfulfilled people, and, because we live in New York, we like to keep it that way.

"Open the bloody door!" shouted a voice from the hallway.

I did not require the services of Professor Higgins to identify the rather singularly accented ejaculations of Mick Brennan. Mick had been born in England of Irish parents and possibly for this reason had experienced some personal confusion about his politics. That personal confusion had grown and evolved to a state where, at times, he hated everyone. Unfortunately, I often understood his feelings a little better than I would've liked.

"Open this bloody fucking door!" shouted Brennan again.

His remarks created a mild degree of disapproval on the part of the cat, as well as engendering a small work stoppage on the parts of Vinnie and Gepetto. The disturbance, very possibly, did not unsettle me as much as the others. All I had to do was take my feet off the desk.

"What're you doing, mate?" said Mick, upon observing the work in progress. "Reenacting *The Diary of Anne Frank*?"

"It's certainly possible," I said.

"You know I saw the play performed in Dublin a few years ago."

"*The Diary of Anne Frank*? How was it?"

"It was dreadful, mate. The acting was bloody awful. By the

time the Germans came marching in, the audience was shouting, 'She's in the attic!'"

"I didn't have an attic until recently," I said, "and I damn sure don't want to know what's in or above it."

"That's good," said Brennan, "because with McGovern as your lead secret undercover agent you're not going to learn a fucking thing. The only thing he's going to accomplish is thoroughly pissing off your upstairs neighbors."

"C'mon, Mick, you've got to give McGovern a little more credit than that."

"*You* give him all the credit you want, mate. I've seen the man in action. I don't know what exactly you told him the other day but the bloke thinks he's James Bond on a mission from God. He's also talking about camping out up there like a cold-war spy or something. You know he won't be up there ten minutes before he's drinking all their booze and hitting on all the birds."

"Hell," I said, feigning a mild, controlled anger. "McGovern's been on the assignment only three days and he's already jeopardizing the confidentiality of the operation. I was crazy to believe he'd make a trustworthy Watson."

"Watson?"

"As in Sherlock Holmes," I said, gesturing toward the porcelain head on my desk.

"I see," said Brennan uncomfortably, looking around the room for some kind of sanity or support.

Vinnie and Gepetto kept on plastering. The cat continued to sleep under her heat lamp. Christ, I thought, what a brilliant fox Brennan would make to watch over the chicken coop. I could just envisage a modern biblical rendering of David meeting Goliath if McGovern got out of hand and Brennan attempted to cut him down to size. No one could intercede in a battle like that. It might rage for days. Until all the Philistines had fled Judaea. I poured Brennan and myself a shot of Jameson's and persuaded him to sit down in the almost perpetually empty client's chair beside the desk. We quickly killed the shots.

"Mick," I said in confidential tones, "did McGovern tell you anything about the note?"

"Never mentioned any note, mate. He was hustling about all hush-hush about every bloody thing, and when McGovern tries to keep something secret it's worse than another bloke shouting it to the bloody winds."

"He does bring a rather singular naïveté to the case."

"With disaster invariably nipping at naïveté's heels."

"You have remarkable insight into the man. Maybe it's just good fortune, but McGovern may very possibly have unintentionally tipped his hand to the one person I could really count on."

"How about another round, mate?" said Brennan, shifting uneasily in his chair.

"Of course."

I poured us each another round. Before we poured the nectar down our necks I made a little toast.

"To friends who can be trusted," I intoned.

"I'll drink to that," said Brennan, as we both downed the shots. "Of course, I'll drink to anything."

The second shot had pretty well hamstrung my uvula. As I waited for my vocal cords to stop ringing in my ears I brought forth yet again the worn-out, weather-beaten threat note that had always done the trick in the past. When something works, stay with it.

"This is the note that the woman upstairs recently received and brought to me. She was, understandably, quite traumatized by the experience."

"You didn't write this yourself, did you, mate?" said Brennan, with a peal of rather perverse laughter.

"Mick," I said, affecting a hopefully convincing blanch, "I'm a private investigator." This, of course, was hardly true. To the

77

Village Irregulars, I was a private investigator. To the cat, I was a private investigator. But to a private investigator, I was no private investigator. To guys like Kent Perkins in L.A., or Rambam, I was just an amateur sleuth dicking around in their business. The same, of course, could undoubtedly have been said about Miss Marple, though in her case, the phrase "dicking around" would probably not be applicable.

"I'm kidding, mate," said Brennan, carefully scouring the note. "This is clearly the handiwork of one very dodgy motherfucker."

Again I felt the slight urge to defend the note, but I thought better of it. There's probably a little bit of Idi Amin and a little bit of Mother Teresa in all of us. About the only thing we can truly be thankful for is that the two of them never decided to have any children.

"I need you, Watson," I said, perhaps a bit overdramatically. "I need you. I promised Winnie Katz, she runs the lesbian dance upstairs—"

"McGovern alluded to that."

"I'm sure he did. At any rate, I promised her I'd say nothing to anyone about the note and take no action regarding it. But I feel I have to do something. Her life could be in danger."

"With McGovern up there, everyone's life could be in danger."

"You're the perfect Watson, Mick. You can keep an eye on McGovern, keep me informed, and Winnie will never suspect that the game's afoot. If trouble should start, I'm sure you'll know how to handle it."

I had to smile at this point because if there was a more accomplished troublemaker in the world than Mick Brennan, I'd never met him. God had put Brennan on this earth to cause trouble, and Mick, with a lifetime of experience under his belt, was now the best in the business.

"Out with the old Watson," I said, as I firmly took Mick's hand in mine, "in with the new!"

78

"Okay, mate. McGovern's already set up the initial interview for tomorrow afternoon. I'll go innocently along with my camera gear. Maybe while I'm at it I can shoot a little beaver."

"That's the spirit, Watson!"

"One more thing, Sherlock. Do I have to call you Sherlock?"

"That's entirely at your discretion, Watson. Does it bother you?"

"Not really," said Brennan. "It just sounds a bit like a poofter."

13

I T ' s the night before the big game!" I shouted to the cat at two o'clock in the morning. "Everybody get pumped!"

The cat was not even remotely curious about my ill-timed and unseemly display of adolescent enthusiasm. She'd seen it often enough before, no doubt, but she lived in hope that some day a small measure of mature behavior might descend upon my being. I lived in hope that some day a sense of humor might descend upon the cat. Because we live our lives in such hopeless hope is the main reason that cats and people are often so disappointed.

"The players are all ready to take their places," I continued in manic tones, as I paced across the uncluttered portion of the living-room floor. "How could I possibly sleep? I'm nervous as a cat, pardon the expression. I'm as excited as Le Petomane on the night before one of his great performances at the Moulin Rouge."

The cat did not even pretend to share my exhilaration. For one thing, she had never been a fan of Le Petomane. Like one hundred percent of all modern women, she did not find farting to be very humorous. Like one hundred percent of all cats, she did not find anything else to be very humorous either.

"Why can't you be a better sport about all this?" I asked the cat somewhat rhetorically. The question had to be somewhat rhetorical, as the cat was sitting on the desk deliberately with her back to me. If you don't think cats know when you're out where the buses don't run, on booze or drugs, you're wrong. Virtually every time I'd found myself walking on my knuckles, the cat had demonstrated her displeasure in precisely similar fashion. I know this because cats are neurotically curious creatures. If you're the only action in the room, they're going to want to look at you. For a cat to sit erect with its back to you is a better index of your inebriation and/or your insanity than could be determined by you walking a straight line for a cop or having a session with Woody Allen's shrink.

"Yes, I'm having a little fun here," I said to the back of the cat. "A week from now that Medusa upstairs is going to wish she'd only been visited by the twelve plagues of Egypt. And she deserves what she gets. At the rate Vinnie and Gepetto are working, they'll be here until next Purim. And it could get pretty ugly if I have to try to christian Joe the Hyena down on the cost of the job."

From the reaction I got from the cat, I might as well have been talking to the porcelain head of Sherlock Holmes. Not only did the cat like Vinnie and Gepetto and no doubt wish they would stay forever, I sensed that she also might've detected a bit of a vengeful spirit in my merry prankster crusade against Winnie. Part of me, indeed, wondered if I hadn't already gone too far. Had I set so many wheels in motion that one of them, quite accidentally, might take us all away?

"I know what you're thinking," I said to the cat. "Pulling a chair out from under a lesbian is hardly a Gandhi-like thing to do. It's a little like correcting Davy Crockett's table manners. Or poking fun at Kathie Lee Gifford. Or offering Don Imus a

Vodka McGovern. Or sending McGovern to pull a chair out from under a lesbian. Or pulling the world out from under a star-crossed lover."

The cat turned around.

"I know it's tough being a cat in this dog-eat-dog world," I said. "Sherlock's lonely, too. Look at him. Look at me. If there's a real Watson left in this Nike Village we call the nineties we need to find him as soon as possible. If not, we must face a challenge far more difficult and uncertain. Find him in ourselves. But it isn't going to be easy. The fabric of the Judeo-Christian loincloth is wearing a bit thin these days. Hell, I probably would've been a Buddhist if it weren't for Richard Gere."

The cat, by this time, was sound asleep, possibly dreaming of Porsches and bayous and hedgehogs and flamingos, and a quiet little garden in the southern sun. About twenty-seven minutes later, I joined her in the garden.

14

When I woke up bright and early Thursday morning it was already noon. Gary Cooper time. The phones were ringing and Vinnie and Gepetto were banging on the door of the loft. I collared the blower on the way to the door and without waiting for the caller to identify himself, I merely shouted, "Hold the weddin'!" into the receiver and tossed it on the desk where the cat sat next to it studying it intently.

"We knew you liked to sleep late," said Vinnie when I opened the door, "so we thought we'd give you a break."

"Perfect timing," I said.

"Yeah," said Gepetto. "A passing lesbian let us in the building."

"Perfect timing," I said.

When I got back to the desk the cat was still sitting there listening to the squeaking receiver like the dog in the old RCA commercial.

"That's not your master's voice," I told her brusquely. "You don't have a master."

"MIT . . . MIT . . . MIT," said the blower when I placed it against my left earlobe.

"MIT . . . MIT," I responded.

MIT, which rhymed with SHIT, stood for the Man In Trouble Hotline that McGovern and I had set up exclusively between ourselves some years back and thus far had served no useful purpose whatsoever. The hotline had been established when McGovern saw a story on the wire about a man who'd died in a Chicago apartment and because he had no friends, or possibly because he had inept, unpredictable friends like the Village Irregulars, no one realized that he'd stepped on a rainbow and his body lay in state right there in his apartment until it had achieved the approximate consistency of some of your finer frog pâtés. It was to avoid such an unpleasantness occurring to either of us that the Man In Trouble Hotline had been created. Since McGovern and I had no spouses, no live-in lovers, no maids, no children, no doormen, no offices, no bosses, no bowling partners, and no ability to regulate the chaos that was our lives, it sounded like a reasonable way to occasionally check each other's pulse. Of course, McGovern did have an advantage over me. His body wasn't going to be eaten by a cat.

"I can't find that fucking Brennan," McGovern shouted. "I've got the first interview with Winnie set up for this afternoon. I told her it was a three-part series for the *Times* of London on 'The Evolution of Dance.' She went for it totally. Now Brennan's pulled a disappearing act."

"Start without him if necessary. Who's running this undercover operation anyway?"

"*I* am."

"Right you are, Watson. By the way, where are you calling from?"

"I'm calling from a hi-tech specialty shop called 'I Spy.' I'm getting a tiny recording device that can be concealed on my body."

"Good thinking, Watson! You might pick up a new magnifying glass for me while you're down there."

"I'll report back later, Sherlock."

"By the way, Watson. It might be best to keep in touch by phone. It won't do to have you spotted coming into my flat by a passing lesbian."

"No one sees The Shadow," said McGovern. "But The Shadow knows."

"Very good, Watson," I said, as I cradled the blower.

"Very sick, Watson," I said to myself, as I rummaged around in Sherlock's head for a fresh cigar.

I lit my first cigar of the day and kicked the espresso machine into gear. It hissed and gurgled and had just begun to hum a pretty fair rendition of "Happy Talk" from *South Pacific* when the phones rang again. It certainly had the makings of a very busy day, but there's nothing you can't handle if you know how to delegate. I walked over to the desk, sat down, puffed rather pontifically on the cigar a few times, and lifted the blower on the left.

"Start talkin'," I said.

"Houston," said Mick Brennan, "we have a problem. I can't find that fucking McGovern."

I winked at the cat and puffed peacefully on the cigar for a few moments. They didn't call them the Village Irregulars for nothing, I thought.

"He's down at some spy shop purchasing a tiny, hi-tech recording device that can be concealed on his body."

Brennan laughed for some little period of time. I chuckled along with him good-naturedly. It would be a tragic mistake for someone in my position to take sides.

"A large, old-fashioned, reel-to-reel tape recorder could be concealed on McGovern's body," said Brennan. "A giant bloody satellite dish that picks up signals from outer space could be concealed on McGovern's bleeding body."

"Watson, Watson," I said, striving for just the properly patronizing tone, "this is so unlike you, my dear Watson."

"Now you're really starting to sound like a poofter, mate."

"Where the hell do you think you're going, Brennan?" I said, momentarily losing a bit of my composure. "There's a whole dance class full of poofters up there."

"But they're female poofters. They don't lisp when they say 'Sherlock Holmes.'"

"Ah, Watson, as always your keen mind misses very little in this blind, uncaring, trivial world."

"Sod the blind, uncaring, trivial world," said Brennan. "I've got all this bloody gear ready to go. What the bleedin' hell am I supposed to do with it besides shovin' it up McGovern's arse when I find him?"

"Why not start without McGovern, Watson? The early bird gets the worm."

"And then the worm gets all the rest of us, mate."

"Rather morbid, Watson. Quite unlike you to sound so morbid."

"Morbid," said Brennan, "is what's going to happen when I get my bloody hands on McGovern."

Before I could even give him a few pip-pips of encouragement, Brennan had disengaged the line. Things appeared to be moving along remarkably well. If past experience was any guide, Brennan and McGovern alone were forces to be reckoned with. When these forces collided, a prolonged and memorable explosion usually occurred. Taken in tandem, they could've probably created a breach of etiquette at the Boston Tea Party.

I walked over to the espresso machine and whistled a little tune along with it as I drew a cup of the hot, bitter, black liquid that helped the Romans take over the world. Vinnie and Gepetto, two descendants of that ancient bloodline, gathered around the huge, shiny dingus for their first of about twenty-seven espresso breaks.

"Ain't heard much from upstairs lately," said Vinnie.

"Don't worry," I said. "You will."

86

15

JESUS Christ was the first Texas Jewboy. Of course, Texas had not been invented yet, but it surely existed in the vast, hot, dusty wanderings of the Israelites, not to mention the similarity of spiritual climate between looking for a manger in Bethlehem and finding a hotel room in Dallas. It's also true that if you put cowboy hats and colorful bandanas on Jesus' loyal, zealous, somewhat eccentric disciples, they all would tend to look and act like Gabby Hayes.

This is not to take anything away from the great Gabby Hayes, who was overworked, underfucked, and underappreciated in his time, and went on to be overshadowed by his younger brothers, Ira, Isaac, and Woody, and, of course, his sister, Helen. Even his illegitimate stepchild, Purple Haze, conceived on a curious one night stand with Josephine Baker in Waco, Texas, went on to eclipse his father. Roy Rogers, by the way, had always counseled Gabby about the joys of penetrating the man-made, arbitrary barriers between the races of the earth.

"We're all God's children," Roy reportedly had said. "You gotta split that ol' black oak, mate."

"Are you sure this is right?" Gabby had asked.

"Mandatory, my boy, mandatory," Roy had answered, after his well-intentioned, yet somewhat paternalistic fashion.

But getting back to Jesus, as we all find ourselves doing now and then, it must be noted that being King of the Jews, along with all the obvious perks, also requires a rather tedious amount of personal responsibility. Sometimes this becomes too much even for self-effacing types like Jesus and provokes minor outbursts such as the one immediately following the Last Supper, when Jesus is reported to have yelled at the waiter: "Separate checks, please."

The only disciple who eventually hosed Jesus, unless you want to count Paul's rather Madison Avenue approach to things, was Judas, who looked nothing like Gabby Hayes, eschewed chicken-fried steak, collected matchbooks from various upscale restaurants, and bore an almost uncanny resemblance to Andrew Cunanan, without, of course, the Versace jacket.

The above information may strike some as rather outlandish but in fact is the gospel. I know this because I spoke to Jesus about it personally right after he got off the phone with Jerry Falwell and just before he did a satellite hookup interview with the Promise Keepers. Jesus told me, and this provided me with great inner strength, that He was only the first in a long line of historical Jewish troublemakers. After His death, while the disciples were busy discipling, He secretly passed the sacred torch to Spinoza, then to Freud, and then to Karl and Groucho Marx.

This first batch of Jewish troublemakers, though their approaches varied radically, pleased Jesus immensely. Spinoza, who also had a beard like Gabby Hayes, was quite the pointy-headed intellectual and believed that all man's problems could be solved philosophically. Even Jesus realized this was ridiculous. Freud, by this time having consumed a great deal of Irving Berlin's White Christmas, believed there was a Freudian answer to everything. Indeed, his pubic hair was said to resemble

Gabby Hayes's beard. Karl Marx, who also had a beard like Gabby's, passionately contended that all of mankind's troubles could be solved politically. Jesus had to laugh at that one. "Tell that to Gary Hart," he'd reportedly commented at the time.

Groucho was the only one of this early group that I got to meet face-to-face after we were introduced in a men's room in New York by Maureen Orth. Groucho was just a step away from the Shalom Retirement Village at the time, but, as we urinated next to each other, his wit and wisdom shimmered through.

"I've already met everyone I want to meet," he said. "The only advice I can give you is this: Go back to Texas."

In due course, I followed Groucho's advice. But first, the two of us had to finish bleeding our lizards and then complete the process of ritually washing our hands three times. On the way out of the men's room, there occurred one more little snippet of conversation. It was a small thing really, but as the years have passed, I've pondered over it often and it might not be inappropriate to say that it has greatly affected my attitude concerning the mortal nature of man and of his purpose here on earth.

"Where are you going?" I asked Groucho.

"I'm going home to bend one into my wife," he said.

The second batch of latter-day Jewish troublemakers who were direct, though possibly totally oblivious, descendants of the Holy Spirit were Jack Ruby, Lenny Bruce, Abbie Hoffman, and Joseph Heller. Jack Ruby was a very colorful fellow who woke me up from sleeping through my entire first year of college by croaking Lee Harvey Oswald, who'd recently croaked President Kennedy from the fourth floor of the Texas Cookbook Suppository Building, which was located in either Dallas or Bethlehem at the time, take your pick. The greatest thing Jack Ruby ever did, however, was to be one of the last, loyal friends, along with Bill Monroe, that Hank Williams ever had. Ruby believed that the most important thing a man could do was to regularly attend any one of the burlesque nightclubs he ran in Dallas, and Jack, in this regard, quite unintentionally may have come the closest of anybody to alleviating the problems of mankind.

Lenny Bruce possibly lived his life in the truest imitation of Christ the world has ever seen. He was skinny, he was Jewish, he was misunderstood, and he fully grasped the nobility of suffering. In death, as well as life, Lenny continued his conscious campaign to be cryptically Christ-like. Jesus died nailed to a cross between Dismas and Barabbas, two thieves. Bruce died on a toilet with a needle in his arm. Between the gutter and the stars, the windmill and the world, the commode and the cross, there has never been a noticeably significant spiritual distance.

Abbie Hoffman, the seventh Jewboy ordained by the God of the Hebrews, was destined to wander political, cultural, and spiritual deserts of America for most of his years. He was the clown prince of the celestial school who, like Lenny, was one of the first Americans to quite literally wrap himself in the American flag, long before it became sartorially fashionable. It is no accident that his name was Abraham. It is also no accident that his flesh-and-blood son was named america. But in very many ways, Abbie could be considered today to be the crazed, charismatic, yet idealistic father of the surviving, salient sensibilities we now think of as the sixties. He was born on the Fourth of July, but his spirit is resurrected anytime anyone anywhere questions authority. Abbie did wear a Gabby Hayes beard sometimes. At other times he wore other disguises. And Abbie, of course, rhymes with Gabby.

The last troublemaking Jewboy on the list, thank Christ, is Joseph Heller, the author of *Catch-22*, a book that, though it hasn't caused as many deaths as the Bible, has at least occasionally caused people around the world to stop and think about the nature of life. Heller operates on two basic principles: "Nothing succeeds as planned" and "Every change is for the worse." If you model your life on Heller's principles you can't go wrong, and if you do, you probably won't realize it. Joseph Heller is considered by many religious authorities to be the only living direct disciple of Jesus. I take this on faith, though biblical scholars have recently produced at least two pieces of physical evidence to support this contention. One: His white, unruly hair looks incredibly similar to one of the lesser biblical prophets named Hymie who predicted that Jews would never play golf. And two: The name "Joseph Heller" has the same first two initials as Jesus H. Christ. Working against Heller's place in history, of course, is the fact that he doesn't have a beard like Gabby Hayes.

There are other Jews who've stirred the putrefying pot of human history down through the years, but they don't leap to mind. In fact, they don't leap anywhere because most of them have been killed by well-intentioned, fanatical Christians, possibly not unlike yourself, kindred in nothing but name, who believed *they* were doing the Lord's work by sponsoring the Crusades, the Inquisition, and the Holocaust. Alan Dershowitz touches upon this issue in one of his recent books, *The Vanishing American Jew,* which misled many of us into the false hope that it was autobiographical.

But Jesus never meant for any of this to happen. He was a good Jewish boy. He just wanted people to be nice. He doesn't have the time or the interest to bother communicating with statesmen or generals or Christian athletes or good little church workers or televangelists or people who call radio stations quoting scripture or flocks of faithful who read the Bible so they can pass the final exam or Brother Oralingus or Brother Analingus or Billy Graham or you or me or any other ambulatory nerd enjoying the fruits of the land. Jesus speaks regularly to only one group of people. They are the people in mental hospitals. They try to tell us, but we never believe them.

These are the kinds of thoughts that go through your head if you smoke enough Cuban cigars and keep your feet propped up on your desk for fifty-three years. They're dangerous thoughts because some of them may turn out to be true.

16

"Dickhead."

"Start talkin'."

"That's *so* cornball. Can't you just answer the phone like a normal person?"

"Why?"

"Because if you'd answered the phone like a normal person I might've shown you what I look like in these sexy black tights."

"Friedman residence. To whom am I speaking, please?"

"Too late, asshole. I'm going across the hall now. If I'm still heterosexual when I get back, I'll give you a call."

"Stephanie, just be careful. It's not worth—"

But she'd already cradled the blower. I looked past the slow-moving forms of Vinnie and Gepetto into the gray, dying afternoon and I began to have some mixed feelings about this frivolous little venture. Suppose Stephanie *did* become gay? It'd certainly happened before, possibly in precisely this same fashion. What if my little scheme backfired and somebody got hurt or arrested? What if the operation was such a successful disaster that Winnie lost her livelihood, had a complete nervous breakdown, and was hauled off to wig city by burly dykes in white nurse's uniforms? Maybe she'd like it. Maybe she wouldn't. Maybe she'd take a Brodie in wig city and her blood would be on my hands for the rest of my life as I languished here in the loft immersed in a terrible, guilt-ridden silence wishing only that it could be broken by something human and real like a lesbian dance class. Maybe I'd lose all my friends when they discovered how I'd duped them with the threat note and seduced them into thinking they were the perfect Watson. Maybe there was no perfect Watson. Maybe there was no Watson at all. Maybe it was just me and the cat and the puppet head. Maybe everybody in the world was working without a net.

"Start talkin'," I said, as I robotically hoisted the blower on the left.

"Kinkstah!" said the loud, familiar, irritating voice. "I've got it!"

"What've you got, Ratso? A dead man's catcher's cup?"

"I may need one when this is over."

"We all may need one when this is over. I'm rather busy today, Watson. What is it you wished to tell me?"

"I've got the plan! The plan for going undercover into the lesbian dance class!"

"That's great, Rats. What is it?"

"I'd rather not divulge it just yet."

"Watson, you're the soul of discretion. You're nothing if not controlled, cautious, and very likely constipated. Now what the hell's the plan?"

"I'm not kidding, Sherlock. I'd rather just keep it to myself until I see if it actually works."

"Good thinking, Watson! Better safe than sorry, old boy."

"I knew you'd understand, Sherlock."

"There may well be an international cartel of lesbians who right at this moment through sophisticated satellite spying techniques are monitoring this very call. Even if they don't, you can't trust anybody these days, Watson. Not even one of your closest fucking friends."

"I knew you'd understand, Sherlock."

"I'll never understand you, Ratso. That's part of your charm."

"If there're some good-looking lesbians in the class, I may be hanging out there for quite a while. Some of them have probably never been with a man before. Maybe I can work on them and change their minds about things."

"Ah, Watson, you're quick as ever in perceiving the opportunities life may throw your way. I have no doubt that you'll charm them out of their little lesbian leotards. Just as you've charmed me once again with this phone call."

"Okay, Kinkstah! My secret plan goes into operation this evening. Wish me luck!"

"Good luck."

"He's going to need more than good luck," I said to the cat as I cradled the blower. "If there's one thing any self-respecting lesbian hates it's a crude, loud, weirdly dressed, abrasive nerd like Ratso who thinks he's the Don Juan of Lower Manhattan. I have an image of him pertinaciously plying his charms on some surly bull dyke with a tool belt."

The cat, of course, said nothing in response to my provocative remarks. She knew that I often made hasty, ill-thought-out comments when I got off the blower with Ratso. She knew, also, that I would soften in my attitude toward the man who would be Watson very possibly because of his, for want of a better word, charm. Ratso, indeed, was not without charm. It was just that he had such a thoroughly obnoxious charm delivery system that by the time its influence took effect he'd managed to totally repel you forever.

The cat despised Ratso and made no secret of it. She'd harbored a hatred for him since the first time he'd walked into the loft and promptly become a housepest for about six months. It was an irrational kind of thing, as I often pointed out to her, but there it was. The cat liked Rambam, who was half-Italian, and she liked Vinnie and Gepetto. Maybe she had a thing for Italians. She tolerated McGovern, was oblivious to Brennan, and probably would've liked Stephanie DuPont if it weren't for her two little dogs, Pyramus and Thisbe, ice-picking everybody's brains out all the time with their loud, sharp, incessant yipping and yapping.

One cannot humor a cat totally in regard to one's interpersonal relations and expect to have many friends in this world. Cats are like lesbians. They are creatures of narrow habit about which men can only glimpse the silken machinery of their minds. If people are ever truly beautiful, however, it is because of who and what they are and we must never try to change that. Let cats be cats. Let rats be rats. Let lesbians be lesbians. Let little dogs be little dogs. And let us pray that all of them are never present in the same place at the same time. If that truly tedious circumstance ever occurs, let us at least hope that Vinnie and Gepetto have finished their work on my ceiling.

I was about ready to take a late-afternoon break from what had been a busy day at the office, when the phones rang again. I puffed peacefully on a cigar and let them ring for a while. The plan was in motion and nothing but an act of God, Buddha, Allah, or Pat Robertson was going to stop it now. Besides, I figured, the last thing you want anybody in New York to think is that you've got time on your hands. Blood on your hands, people can learn to accept. Time on your hands, forget it. After the twin blowers had pretty well blown out my inner ear, I plucked the left blower and planted it on the side of my face.

"Church of the Transfiguration," I said. "Father Friedman speaking."

"Fuck yourself, Father Friedman," said a gruff voice that I eventually recognized as Rambam's.

"That's a hell of a way to speak to a man of the cloth."

"The only way you'd know anything about the cloth is if your relatives worked in the garment district in Texas."

"They did. But until they found out about Calvin Klein, they just used to run around naked."

"Calvin Klein probably would've liked that. Look, I finished the Jewish lightning case faster than I thought, so I'll drop over to see you and then I'll bug Winnie's place later tonight."

"Don't you think she might be suspicious with you coming in at night?"

"Hey," said Rambam, "Con Ed never sleeps."

Several hours later, as Vinnie and Gepetto were packing up to leave, Rambam came in carrying a flashlight and a clipboard with some kind of crazy-looking meter hooked onto his belt. He was wearing a Con Ed cap, a Con Ed shirt, and a rather mischievous smile.

"Didn't know you worked for Con Ed," said Vinnie to Rambam.

"I don't," said Rambam.

"I'll let you in on a little secret," said Gepetto. "We don't belong to the International Brotherhood of Electrical Workers either."

"And since Kinky here's not a real detective," said Rambam with a leer, "the only one who's legit in the place is the cat."

"That's good to know," said Vinnie, leaving a few cannolis on the counter as he and Gepetto headed out the door.

"Where'd you get that weird-looking device you're wearing on your belt?" I asked, when the two workmen had gone.

"It's on loan from the Sex Crimes Unit," said Rambam.

"Don't forget to take it back," I said.

"For your edification," said Rambam, "it's a rather medieval device called a phyzagometer. They strap it on the schlongs of sex offenders and then show them porno flicks to test whether or not they should remain on parole."

"If you think you're testing it on me, you're very much mistaken."

"That was the last thing on my mind. I'm going to persuade

your neighbors upstairs that it's the newest thing in gas-leak detection. If there's one piece of equipment no lesbian in the world would recognize it's the phyzagometer."

"Makes sense. Where's the transmitter for the listening device?"

"It's built into this pager," said Rambam, holding a normal-looking pager in the palm of his hand. "All I plan to do is toss it under a sofa or some piece of heavy furniture when the lovely little lesbians aren't looking. Should transmit for at least a week or two."

If McGovern doesn't step on it, I thought. I blew a purple plume of cigar smoke upward toward the ceiling and inadvertently studied the ongoing plastering job.

"You know," I said, "Vinnie and Gepetto *are* beginning to make some progress."

"That's encouraging," said Rambam, "because you can't exactly fire guys who work for Joe the Hyena. All right, if there's nothing else, I'm going up. I'll drop off the receiver with you on my way down."

"Hold the weddin', Rambam. If the transmitter's in the pager, where's the receiver?"

"In the phyzagometer," said Rambam.

"That'll send your penis to Venus," I said.

Rambam was halfway to the door when an enormous crashing noise occurred directly over our heads. It sounded like John Tesh and his piano had just been dropped by a crane. The cat scurried under the desk for cover. The little black puppet head rattled around on top of the refrigerator.

"What the hell was that?" I asked, not entirely sure I wanted to know the answer.

"Just be glad the phyzagometer wasn't receiving yet," said Rambam. "That one would've blown out your fucking windows."

17

WHILE I waited for Rambam to plant the bug in Winnie's loft, I shared a bit of Vinnie's cannoli with the cat and poured myself a few stiff shots from the bottle of El Jimador tequila that my friend Perla had recently sent from Mexico. Cannoli and tequila are not for everyone. If you have all your taste buds intact, this culinary speedball could present a problem. But if you're an experienced, somewhat cosmopolitan person who's smoked cigars for over twenty years, not only is this a killer-bee combination, but it also can give you quite a little buzz.

It seemed to be taking Rambam a bit longer upstairs than I'd anticipated. It couldn't take much time, I figured, to toss a pager under a sofa and get the hell out of there. On the other hand, if you've ever hung around waiting for a Con Ed guy to show up, you're no doubt aware that the tedium and frustration of the experience very nearly surpasses that of waiting for a lover who's never coming back. It's almost as hard, so I've been told, as pretending to look out a window while your wife is crying.

"Did I ever tell you," I said to the cat, "why big-game hunters almost invariably have sexual dysfunctions?"

The cat did not respond, but it was easy to see that I'd piqued her interest. I was pacing back and forth in the kitchen, smoking a cigar, and preparing to elaborate on my subject matter, when Rambam came bursting in the door.

"Didn't your mother ever teach you to knock?" I said, when the cat and I had recovered what was left of our composure.

"Not after witnessing the terrifying vision I just encountered in the hallway. It's lucky for you I didn't strip naked, attach the phyzagometer to myself, and go running down the streets."

"What could make a trained PI behave in such a highly agitato manner?" I asked the cat somewhat rhetorically, since Rambam apparently wasn't listening. Instead, he was following the straightest line between the door and the bottle of El Jimador.

"*Licensed* private investigator, I might add," said Rambam, "unlike some other pretenders to the throne I could mention."

"You're making me nervous. I may have to use the throne if you don't tell me pretty damn quickly what happened."

"Okay," said Rambam, pouring himself a tall shot of tequila. "But I think you'd better be sitting down when you hear this."

"That bad, is it?"

"Worse than the most horrifying cocaine-induced nightmare you've ever had in your life."

"Impossible!" I said.

Rambam rapidly poured the shot of tequila down his neck and gasped for air like a prehistoric fish. The cat watched with a stern glare of disapproval in her eyes.

"Jesus Christ," said Rambam. "How can your mind function after drinking this shit?"

"Impossible!" I said, as I walked over and sat in the chair by the desk. "Suppose you sit down as well and just calmly take it from the top."

Rambam proceeded to sit down across from me and organize his scattered thoughts. From the look on his face, which was now whiter than a Klansman's sheets, I could see that he must've had quite a scare.

"First of all," he said, "as pertains to who might've written the threatening note and who might be plotting to do harm to Winnie, you've got to suspect everybody."

"Standard operating procedure, old bean."

"I'll be a refried bean if I keep drinking this El Jimador shit. I mean, suspect *everybody*."

"Okay. Suspect *everybody*. Now get to the meat of it."

"I've got two pieces of bad news for you," said Rambam, "and you may as well hear it now rather than later."

"Spit it," I said, feigning the same serious countenance as Rambam.

"The first thing as I'm going in the place is I run into this big-butch security gal. She kind of works like a Joe Louis–type greeter in reverse. She's unpleasant, unfriendly, and she doesn't want you to come in. I tell her I work for Con Ed, which should be obvious to a moron by my appearance, and I've got to see the tenant of the apartment immediately because of a possible gas leak in the building. This kind of pitch is usually enough to get you in to see the Pope, but this gal wasn't having any.

"She says, 'Ms. Katz cannot be disturbed. She's being interviewed by the *Times* of London.' I say, 'I don't care if she's being interviewed by the *Gap-lapper Gazette*, lady, if there's a gas leak in here and I don't find it, the whole goddamn place'll blow up.' "

"You didn't say that."

"Of course I did."

"And what was her response?"

"She said, and I quote: 'You're cruisin' for a bruisin' from Susan.' "

"Wonderful, Watson, wonderful! Through your clever banter

with this woman you've been able to provide us with her name!"

"What was there to lose? There was a room with the door closed where Winnie was supposedly being interviewed, and if I'd been Alice B. Toklas she wouldn't have let me in there. But I did manage to get past Susan into the main part of the dance studio, and that's where we encounter our first piece of bad news."

"Lay it on me, Alice."

"You're laughing now," said Rambam. "Just wait. So I go into the dance studio part of the loft looking for a place to hide the transmitter and there's about ten girls in there doing stretching exercises or something. I guess they're waiting for Winnie to finish her big interview."

"I'm waiting for you to tell me something I don't know."

"We're getting to that," said Rambam with a rather evil glint in his eye. "So I'm kind of scoping out the group and over on one side I see a tall, statuesque blonde who looks like a god-damn Greek goddess wearing black tights and I do mean tights and I've got sort of a rear view of her, which wasn't bad by the way, but even from that angle she looks kind of familiar. I stare at her for a few moments and then the girl next to her, a not bad-looking redhead actually, starts helping her adjust her leg on the ballet bar. The blonde turns sideways to me, which is also not a bad view, then she looks directly at me, but of course it doesn't register because she thinks I'm a Con Ed guy. But there's no doubt about it. I can't fucking believe it. It's her!"

"It's who?"

"Stephanie DuPont."

"WHAT!"

"I hate to be the one to have to tell you, old pal, but there's about as much chance of you ever scoring with her as there is of your little wooden puppet head turning into a real live boy."

"There's got to be some mistake."

"I'm afraid not. Just be glad you weren't on hand to personally witness the look of ecstasy in Stephanie's eyes as the red-head helped her adjust her leg on the ballet bar."

"I'll kill both of them," I said with some vehemence.

"Spoken like a real man."

"Ah, fuck both of them," I said, allowing my anger to dissolve into bitterness.

"That crossed my mind, too," said Rambam. "Unfortunately, it doesn't look like anybody's going to fuck either of them."

I got up rather dramatically from the desk, walked over to the counter, and poured a stiff shot of El Jimador into the old bull's horn. Then I poured it down my neck. Then I leveled a long, brokenhearted gaze out the window into the brokenhearted New York night.

"All the lesbian dance classes in all of the world," I said, "and Stephanie had to join this one."

"Forget it," said Rambam. It was almost poignant how he was falling for it. But telling him the truth now was out of the question. He probably wouldn't have believed it anyway.

"Show me how to set up the receiver," I said, in brisk tones that indicated I was stoically going on with my life.

"We can set the device right in the middle of your desk and you can turn the volume up or down or on and off just like a radio. It's already working, but the problem is when they're playing dance music that's all you're going to hear."

Rambam put the receiver on the desk, turned up the dial, and the room filled rapidly with what sounded like deconstructed disco. I turned the receiver off.

"Tedious," I said.

"Of course when the music's playing you'll probably want to keep it turned off. Now if you get bored you could always strap it to your penis and find out how you really feel about things."

"Thanks for the household tip. By the way, since this seems to be somewhat of a theme tonight, what's the other piece of bad news?"

"Okay," said Rambam, warming to the subject, "so I've planted the transmitter and I'm walking out the door and just as I'm starting down the stairs the elevator door opens. And guess who's walking out of the elevator and into Winnie's loft?"

"Ellen DeGeneres."

"Not quite. It's a guy mincing along wearing these pathetic pink tights stretched to the breaking point over his fat ass. For the top he's wearing a 'Re-elect Barney Frank' sweatshirt cut off at the sleeves."

"You're kidding."

"I'm not fucking kidding. I'm also not kidding about how totally disgusting his outfit was. You know how there's always one male nerd who joins an all-female aerobics class? I thought this must be the one fagola who's joining the lesbian dance class. He was so excited about going in there he didn't even see me. But when I got a good glimpse of who he was I swear I almost puked."

"Hold the weddin'," I said. "You mean I know this guy?"

"Obviously, not as well as you thought you did."

"So who the hell was it?"

Rambam, indeed, seemed thoroughly disgusted with the incident. The cat appeared to be thoroughly disgusted with the entire human race. Even I was mildly disgusted as I listened to Rambam make the grim pronouncement.

"Ratso," he said.

18

I wasn't the kind of person who let bad news get me down for long. The news, of course, hadn't been quite as bad as Rambam had suspected. In fact, the news was quite funny, almost heartening in a certain rather undefinable way. No question, Ratso had gone a little overboard. Also, I probably could've done without the "look of ecstasy" Rambam had described in Stephanie's eyes when the redhead was helping her adjust her leg on the ballet bar. She was playing a part, I reminded myself, but had the look of ecstasy really been necessary? I knew Stephanie better than almost anybody and I'd only seen a look of ecstasy in her eyes on one occasion. That had been the night at McGovern's several years back. We'd just finished eating a killer-bee Chicken McGovern and we'd found an old recipe from a dead gangster named Leaning Jesus, which had turned out to be a map that would supposedly lead us to Al Capone's buried treasure. We were walking back home through the glittering streets of the Village, when Stephanie'd grabbed me by the lapels of my jacket and shouted: "And I get a third, right?" It was when I said "Yes" that the look of ecstasy had come into her eyes.

In this life, I reflected, it's probably better not to look too deeply into people's eyes or into their motivations. Take any look of ecstasy you can get and don't ask questions. The answers are bound to eventually come whether you want them or not.

At the moment, I wasn't looking for any answers. I was feeling like Machiavelli himself, listening to the phyzagometer with the cat, and exulting in the knowledge that all of the Village Irregulars were doing my bidding, moving like so many little chess pieces, plying the waves of destiny for me like the loyal crew on a ship of fools that would be docking soon at a harbor of harassment for one Winnie Katz.

With Rambam gone, it was a very strange, not unpleasant, sensation, being alone in the loft with the cat, listening to the receiver on the desk. It was almost like living by yourself in the country somewhere listening to an old-time radio show. Lots of little old ladies were probably doing exactly the same thing except that none of them were tuned to the station I was. If you've never spied on anyone in your adult life it's something you might want to look, or at least listen, in on. My situation was a bit like being a little old lady and a bit like belonging to the KGB. Though it was living vicariously, there was a definite frisson to the experience. And living vicariously, I understand, can become extremely addictive. Indeed, there are many who say if you can't live vicariously, why bother living at all?

I wasn't sure I felt quite that strongly about it, but I could certainly see their point. After what seemed like interminable dance music we could now hear the little sighs, personal comments, and private conversations that women often have with one another when no man is present. Unless, of course, you want to count Ratso.

"I'd like to introduce Roscoe Figbiter, girls," we could hear Winnie announcing in strident tones. "While we usually don't allow men in the dance classes for obvious reasons—"

"Shhhh," I said to the cat, who, of course, had said nothing. The phyzagometer was spitting out rather sexy, vicarious laughter from the girls. It was not clear whether it'd been provoked by Winnie's comments or Ratso's reaction to them.

"—I've decided to make an exception, on a temporary basis, for Roscoe. He's a member of the Gay Men's Choir of Manhattan—"

Here a light smattering of applause from the class, followed by Ratso saying, "Thank you so much. I love your energy."

"What bullshit," I said to the cat. The cat did not respond but, in fairness to myself, she rarely responded to cynicism in any of its forms. She looked at the receiver and then at the ceiling. Apparently, she loved their energy, too.

"Roscoe's made something of a hobby researching alternative lifestyles and dance styles and avant-garde cultural institutions and I've provisionally agreed to let him audit the course."

"I thought *we* were auditing the course," I said.

"Do you have any comments or questions, Roscoe," said Winnie, "on anything you've seen so far? Of course, you haven't seen *anything* yet." There were suggestive snickers and several rather ribald asides from various members of the class.

"Well, I can already tell you," said Roscoe Figbiter, "that I'm taking copious notes. It's a little more than a hobby with me actually. I've received several degrees from the University of Wisconsin in Madison in the field of cultural anthropology with a major in dance. I've written monographs on dance and ritual among the Flathead Indians of Montana and the Xhosa of South Africa, as well as others I've encountered in my travels. There are definite tribal influences in what I'm seeing today and it's truly quite remarkable."

"He majored in psychology," I said to the cat. "He dropped out of the Ph.D. program because he claimed a spider bit him on the scrotum."

"All I can say," said Figbiter, "is that I'm totally blown away."

"It'd take Hurricane Iniki to blow him away," I said to the cat.

"I'm currently doing some work under Professor Richard Holmes at The New School—"

"Jesus Christ," I said.

"—he's very generous with his per diems and grants, so I'd like to take the whole class out to John's Pizzeria on Bleecker Street when we're through for tonight."

"That's a very kind offer, Roscoe," said Winnie. "Okay, girls, that's it for today. I've got to stay here and do some major repair work on the antique Gustav Stickley table that the large *Times* of London reporter sat on today."

"Oh no," said a voice in the class. "Can I stay behind and help?"

"Thank you, Stephanie. That would be nice. But he was such a large man and he was terribly apologetic, but it was such a small, fragile table. I'm afraid it's a lost cause."

"We all need our lost causes," said Stephanie. "I'll stay behind."

"And believe me," I said, winking rather lasciviously to the cat, "that's one hell of a behind."

The cat turned her back on me rather abruptly, in an unmistakable gesture of extreme disapproval. She remained in that same stubborn, stolid position, facing away from me, gazing almost directly into Sherlock Holmes's pale gray porcelain eyes.

"You've got a nice behind, too," I said, in a rather ridiculous effort to further irritate her frail feline sensibilities. "I'm not quite that spiritually horny yet but if I keep listening to this lesbian dance class long enough I may get there one of these days. Thank God we've got a phyzagometer in the house."

"Don't forget, girls," called Winnie. "We've got the big photo shoot tomorrow! Three o'clock!"

There were a series of rustling and intimate leotard-removing sounds like you might hear in the private ambience of a lesbian locker room. Obviously, Roscoe Figbiter/aka Ratso had left the building. Maybe I was simply imagining things, but the sounds

I was hearing seemed to be creating a heightened sensuality along with a certain ambivalence inside my own being. Like most red-blooded, heterosexual American men, I really didn't know dick about the secrets of the opposite sex. Or maybe that was all I knew. People are so culturally jaded these days that every beautiful natural setting you see seems to look just like a theme park. Personally, I blame Walt Disney, but it probably goes deeper than that, right into the little heart of our great society. Part of me was rapidly becoming convinced that there are certain things we should never seek to know, one of them possibly being the mysteries of lesbianism. Unfortunately, the part of me that was rapidly becoming convinced of this was not the part of me that could be measured with a phyzagometer.

"Goodbye, Stephanie," hissed the receiver. "You sure you don't want to get together later?"

"No thanks, Gena. But I appreciate your helping me with the balance bar."

"I enjoyed it. You've got a terrific body and you're going to be a terrific—um—dancer."

"Thanks, Gena. I really needed the encouragement. I'll see you tomorrow?"

"Wouldn't miss it for the world. You know, I liked you from the minute I laid eyes on you, Stephanie. Something about the way you walked into the room like you had the world by the balls, pardon the expression."

"Well, thanks, Gena."

"Want me to let you in on a little secret, Stephanie?"

"Sure, Gena."

"I wasn't going to tell you this, but a little voice inside me keeps telling me that I should."

"What is it, Gena?"

"You remind me of my ex-wife."

19

Sometime later, after the receiver had been silent for quite a while, blower traffic began to significantly increase in the loft. By this time, I'd fed the cat, reheated an old take-out order from Big Wong's in which the one-thousand-year-old egg was now seemingly quite a bit older, and changed into my incoming wounded outfit, which consisted of a striped bathrobe that had once belonged to a former brokenhearted boyfriend of a former Miss Texas 1987. Once you get to the stage where you refer to yourself as middle-aged, practically everybody's brokenhearted, so it doesn't make a hell of a lot of difference anymore. Once you get to the one-thousand-year-old-egg stage, of course, you really don't give a damn. Rounding out the outfit was a fluffy pair of house slippers in the shape of armadillos. They'd been given to me long ago by a child, possibly one of my numerous godchildren. If you're a godfather to many children it's usually because people feel sorry for you yet they suspect you'll probably be successful some day. As a famous homosexual once said: "Always the godfather, never the god." I can tell you for certain that after a while, not being the god can get pretty tedious.

At the moment, however, the ship of fools still seemed relatively on course, or off course, if you like. I had a great, abiding faith in the Village Irregulars. If they were just given the time and the opportunity, I felt sure they could drive practically anyone irrevocably out where the buses don't run. Ms. Winnie Katz had as yet no idea at all what she was up against. Once my little army had managed to insinuate itself inside the walls of the city, either the walls were going to come tumbling down, or the folks who lived there were sure as hell going to wish they had.

Like Machiavelli, I was prepared to manipulate the men and women who served me toward ends that only I could see, and sometimes I needed to get out my birdbook and binoculars. Mainly, I wanted to keep each Irregular zealous in his or her pursuit of being the perfect Watson. I also strived to help each of them maintain his somewhat misguided belief that, the game being afoot, each of them was the only Watson in the game. So far, so good. But the days ahead would almost certainly challenge my princely powers.

Rambam had already seen Stephanie and Ratso in Winnie's loft, yet he still hadn't stumbled on my master plan. No doubt, Stephanie had seen Ratso, and surely Ratso had seen Stephanie, and Stephanie had almost certainly seen Rambam. Possibly McGovern and Brennan had been sequestered in a private room for Winnie's big interview with the *Times* of London, but by tomorrow they'd both have to be factored into the equation as well. About the only thing going in my favor was that truth is invariably stranger than fiction. In this case the truth was so ridiculous you could look right at it and not take it seriously. Even I was having trouble taking it seriously as I stood by, ready to handle the expected onslaught of Watsons reporting in on the blower. I shared a good-natured chuckle or two with the cat, found a fresh Cuban cigar inside Sherlock's head, fired it up, and waited for the phones to ring. I didn't have to wait very long.

"Bat phone," I said, as I picked up the blower on the left.

"Kinkstah! You should've heard me! I had those lesbians eating out of the palm of my hand!"

"Ah, Watson, I expected no less. Where are you now?"

"I'm at a pay phone. I'm taking a small group of them out to dinner."

"Yes, Watson. And pray tell me how is John's Pizzeria tonight?"

"Jesus Christ, Sherlock! We *are* at John's Pizzeria! How the fuck could you have figured that out?"

"Quite simple, my dear Watson. We're all creatures of narrow habit. I knew what your basic choices would be. I know Chinatown is too far away, possibly too expensive. I know pizza is the kind of meal that can easily accommodate any number of unexpected diners. I know, in the same way that most nurses are smokers, ignoring the obvious health hazards, most dancers tend to prefer to splurge on the least healthy, most fattening foods. I know that, as a general rule, lesbians like pizza. I know your favorite pizza place is John's Pizzeria on Bleecker Street, quite conveniently located to Winnie's studio. And finally, I know that pizza is cheap, no doubt an appealing attribute for someone like yourself who's ostensibly treating a fairly large group of people."

"Now that you've explained it," said Ratso, in mildly disappointed tones, "I realize that I could've probably figured the whole fucking thing out myself."

"You see, Watson, this is why I am so very reticent about revealing my methods. Once I've revealed them to someone the person invariably says 'I could've figured that out myself.' But he *couldn't* have figured it out himself. He *didn't* figure it out himself. And quite often, he's rather a glib, facile, somewhat superficial thinker, not to mention a total asshole, present company excluded of course, my dear Watson."

"Well, I haven't really had a chance to talk much to Winnie

alone, but I'm really going over big with the girls. In fact, I think I've worked it so *they're* taking *me* to dinner tonight. Lesbians *do* like pizza and it looks like they're going to pick up the check."

"Wonderful, Watson, wonderful! I knew you'd somehow manage to do us proud."

"Yeah, well, there's one thing I didn't want to tell you but I guess I should. You know Stephanie, that hot blonde who lives upstairs from you?"

"Yes, Watson. Go on," I said, with practiced irritation.

"Well, she's joined the lesbian dance class."

"WHAT!"

"Sorry, Sherlock."

I let a suitable period of silence pass, in which I poured a stiff, medicinal shot of Jameson Irish Whiskey into the old bull's horn, poured it down my neck, and winked slyly at the cat. The cat did not wink back. She seemed to be gazing without guile directly into the heart of the deception my soul appeared to be effortlessly weaving.

"Easy come, easy go," I said finally, in sadder but wiser tones.

"Don't worry, Sherlock. I'll get to the bottom of this. I'll find out who's got it in for Winnie. Besides, I think a couple of these lesbians are starting to hit on me."

"Careful, Watson! Careful and cautious in matters of the heart. We must maintain a rational distance and a scientific approach."

"I've got a scientific approach, but I'm not so sure about the rational distance. Just give me a little time."

"Time's the money of love, Watson. The money of love."

"Speaking of money," said Ratso, "I've got to get back and make sure the lesbians are picking up the check."

No sooner had the first Watson disengaged the line, than the second Watson began causing my twin red telephones to ring rather clamorously. I picked up the blower on the left.

"Scientology Headquarters," I said. "How can we help you become more like us?"

"Afraid you can't, mate," said Brennan. "Now as for McGovern, he's screwed up already, mate. Bloody near blew our cover."

"That's all right, Watson. Don't worry about the antique table. Was it a Gustav Stickley by any chance? And proceed with the photo shoot tomorrow afternoon as planned."

"You *are* a bleeding Sherlock Holmes. I know you haven't talked to McGovern, because he's had about eight Vodka Mc-Governs and I've been his minder the whole time, getting him safely home and to bed. He was out cold when I left. Done enough damage for one day, I reckon. Probably dreaming right now about how he's going to fuck things up tomorrow. So how'd you know about the table and the photo session? Who told you? By the way, your mate Ratso's a poofter."

"WHAT!"

"Sorry I had to break it to you but you'd probably find out for yourself one of these days in a hot tub or on a camping trip together—"

"Unlikely, Watson. Highly unlikely."

"But I don't think even Ratso knew about the antique table or the photo shoot."

"Watson, Watson, Watson. When will you learn? No one told me a thing about what transpired today. The antique table and the photo shoot are the rather obvious results of a chain of deductive reasoning. As far as the table's concerned—*was* it a Gustav Stickley? I've done some research on antiques in this area and it almost certainly would've been Gustav Stickley unless it was possibly Vagina de Borracho but that would be more prevalent in the Southwest."

"The bloody bitch was complaining about Gustav Stickley—"

"Ah, we have confirmation, Watson. I heard the sound of the disaster and intuited that a large man, McGovern being the only one I knew to be up there, had sat upon a small, fragile, almost assuredly antique table. The sound created by the distance of his large, white, luminous buttocks falling to the wooden floor told me it was no chair. Lesbians themselves, regardless of what man may think of them, are creatures of taste in matters of decor. Also it is known to me that McGovern, if left to his own devices, will hone in on one's most valuable possession and, quite unintentionally, absolutely destroy it.

"The photo session was easier. I knew from the rhythms of the past upon what's left of my ceiling that no photo shoot had occurred today. Though I'm not a photographer like yourself and make no claims to your brilliance in that rarefied field of endeavor, I have researched lighting possibilities in lofts in lower Manhattan to a great degree of detail. I know you would prefer to work in the afternoon light, and judging from past numbers of dancing feet, that would also be the time Winnie would have the whole class present."

"Bloody fucking amazing, Sherlock! If you don't mind me calling you that."

"Anything for you, Watson. Anything for you."

"One more thing, Sherlock. I think I'm beginning to get an idea of who might've written that threatening note to Winnie Katz."

"Speak up, Watson. Your intuitions, as always, are invaluable to me."

"For my money," said Brennan, "it was McGovern."

20

I f you're thinking it's easy being Sherlock Holmes and field-
ing the frailties and foibles of five different Watsons, you'd be
wrong. Endemic in the character of Watson are the myriad pec-
cadilloes of mankind. Ah, how easy it is to be Watson. But being
Sherlock is like being the dog that didn't bark at the Red
Headed League that didn't exist. If you're Sherlock, you're
lonelier than Sergeant Pepper. You're old enough to realize;
young enough to know. You're weak enough to be afraid;
strong enough to let it show. But you're weary because sooner
or later you get tired of suspecting everybody. Then you grow
hideously disillusioned. Then you become totally paranoid.
Then men come and take you away to wig city, where you wind
up masturbating like a monkey in the same cell with Napoleon
and a man from Uranus. And then, as if that weren't enough,
Jesus starts talking to you.

I must've nodded off briefly, because I woke with a start to
find the phones ringing, my feet propped up on the desk, and a
cold, half-smoked cigar still clutched comfortably in my right
hand. If you suspect you may be nodding out a lot, Cuban cigars

are your best bet because they go out very easily and, of course, as Winston Churchill has already previously mentioned, "they're gamier when resurrected." So, no doubt, would be Winston Churchill. I snagged the blower on the left.

"Naval Observatory," I said. "Rear Admiral Rumphumper speaking."

"You know, I've been thinking," said a voice I instantly detected to be Rambam's, "about your situation with the clam diggers upstairs."

"And what have you been thinking, O Oracle of Brooklyn?"

"I'm thinking this may well be an inside job."

My feet involuntarily came off the desk and the unlit cigar almost fell from my fingers, but I made a neat recovery. Rambam already lamping to the fact it might've been an inside job was a little too close to home.

"Watson, Watson, Watson," I said. "Whatever would I—"

"Fuck all this Watson crap," said Rambam in a slightly irritated manner. "In the real world of criminal activity, almost nothing happens in a vacuum. Whoever wrote that note, if he really has it in for Winnie Katz, will probably soon attempt to deliver on his promises. He wants to see her suffer so he will want to witness the misbegotten fruits of his labors. Unless the note is a complete hoax, which under the circumstances I doubt, we can expect further action at any time from the perpetrator."

"Beats watching *Seinfeld*," I said.

"Anything beats watching *Seinfeld*."

"Not quite anything. How about watching Ratso eat pizza? He called me a while ago. He went out for pizza and took some of his lesbian classmates with him. They, I'm told, picked up the check."

"You know, that bothers the hell out of me."

"Lesbians picking up the check?"

"No. Your friend Ratso."

116

"Ratso's behavior bothers me, too. Of course, it always has, come to think of it. But he seems to be making no secret of his involvement with the lesbian dance class or his newfound gay proclivities. It's funny how well you think you can know a guy and then something like this happens."

"That's not what I'm talking about. There probably isn't one living soul on this whole fucking planet who gives a shit if Ratso wants to explore his sexuality, except, of course, the poor schmuck he's exploring it with, whom I do feel sorry for. No one's ever going to 'out' Ratso, because nobody cares. Whether he's in the closet or out of the closet is a matter of total indifference to the world. What's one more guy at South Beach wearing a Versace banana-hammock?"

"I see your point," I said, in an exaggeratedly peevish tone. "You don't have to bite my head off."

"Obviously, you *don't* see my point," said Rambam. "The mating habits of a Jewish middle-aged meatball are not important here."

"Keep me out of it, will you?"

Rambam laughed for the first time in about seventeen years. Then he quieted down a bit. Then he spoke rather grimly. "I'm just trying to tell you," he said, "that I've handled a lot of cases over the years. And right now, the way I see it, your number-one suspect is Ratso."

"Makes sense if you think about it," I said to the cat after Rambam had hung up. The cat came over to the desk, curled up in the middle of it, and closed her eyes.

"Obviously, you don't want to think about it," I said. "That's the trouble with people and cats these days. They can't take a fucking joke. Of course, cats never could take a fucking joke."

The cat opened one yellow eye that was as old as the world. The look she gave me confirmed all my previous sentiments. Then she closed the eye at just about the precise moment the two phones sprang to life, one jangling red machine on either side of her humorless, unforgiving universe. The cat performed a Roger Miller double back flip and scurried off the desk. In the excitement, I dropped my cigar, which this time was lit, and incredibly, it lodged itself between one of my furry armadillo-shaped slippers and the instep of my left foot. It was household accident #247.

I did the best I could to retrieve the cigar before I burned the shit out of myself and I damn near succeeded. Unfortunately, the accident had left a burn mark on the armadillo that resembled something you might have seen on a motel couch in the fifties. Though in some minor pain, I made a last-minute stab for the blower on the left.

"Dr. Felch's office," I said. "The doctor is in."

"Why are you out of breath, dickhead?" asked Stephanie.

"It's not what you think," I said. "I wasn't freeing the hostages. When the phones rang, the cat did a double back flip and I dropped a lit cigar inside one of my armadillo house slippers, receiving a minor burn on my left instep and leaving a burn like you might've seen on a couch of a motel room in the fifties."

"I wasn't around in the fifties."

"No, but your eyes are the color of the motel swimming pool."

"You're a sick man, Friedman. You really are."

"That's the breaking news?"

"Hanging around in your loft with your sick cat and the WPA project those guys are doing on your ceiling. Did they show up today?"

"They don't work on weekends," I said. "Neither do I."

"That's because you never work. But I, fortunately for you, am imbued with a healthy Protestant work ethic and I've practically solved the case while you've been lying around on your ass."

"Ah, Watson, I knew you'd be the one to shed some light into the Riddle of Flatbush Manor."

"I like Winnie. She's odd, eccentric, opinionated, talented, domineering at times. She's a bit like a certain hebe I know, except she doesn't smoke a smelly cigar or wear a cornball cowboy hat. Just because she won't tell you anything doesn't mean she's not going to talk to me. It's a woman thing."

"It certainly is, Watson."

"And while we're on it, let's nip this stupid Watson shit in the bud, all right?"

"All right. I guess 'Twatson' is out of the question."

"Friedman, I'm warning you! One more like that and I'm putting you on social probation and not speaking to you for a month. Then you'll never get this solved."

"We *must* solve it! It's the most baffling adventure I've undertaken since I found the missing crown jewels for the Queen of Upper Baboon's Asshole!"

"Where'd you find them, dickhead?"

"Lower Baboon's Asshole!"

"There's already enough queens and assholes hanging around with just you and Ratso. Or should I say Ratso and you? You want to know who I think's behind this caper, it's your PI pal Rambam, the one who's usually running around with a satellite dish on his head. He was up there scoping out all the girls today, wearing Con Ed drag."

"You're kidding."

"I'm serious as colon cancer. I spotted him right away, of course, but I pretended I didn't recognize him. I strongly advise you to check him out."

"I'll hop right on it."

"In the meantime, guess what? I'm getting a new dog."

"What happened? Did a garbage truck back over Pyramus and Thisbe?"

"Shut up, asshole. She's a three-month-old adorable Maltese who weighs about one and three quarters of a pound. I'll bring her down to meet you next week. You ought to at least say hello, since you're paying for half of her."

"How much is half that doggie in the window?"

"Five hundred dollars."

"Five hundred dollars! That's five grams of cocaine! That's a box of Cuban cigars! That's—"

"Her name's Baby Savannah, and when you see her you'll fall in love with her. She was just this little white ball of fluff sitting in the back of this limo in the lap of a rather fey young man. Her eyes were like two little black buttons and she saw me looking at her and I could hear her little voice inside my head saying, 'You look like a girl who knows how to have fun! Please save me! Save me from a life in the show ring!' So I asked the guy how much he'd take for her and he said a thousand bucks and we're taking her."

" 'Save me from a life in the show ring'?"

"That's what she said."

"I don't know what Vinnie and Gepetto are going to think about me having half ownership in a baby Maltese."

"Who are Vinnie and Gepetto? Your imaginary childhood friends?"

"I never had any imaginary childhood friends. Come to think of it, I've never had any friends. No one's ever given me a chance. Do you think it could be because I go around farting like a bagpiper or do you think it might have something to do with the fact that I've been drinking my own urine like that holy man in India—"

"Who are Vinnie and Gepetto?"

"They're two extremely slow-moving Italian workmen who I hope will have my ceiling fixed in time for Baby Savannah's bas mitzvah party."

"Half ownership doesn't necessarily mean the dog's going to grow up to be a hebe."

"You see, that's the problem with interfaith marriages. Why don't we just let the dog decide?"

"I hope the dog decides to bite your ass."

120

"By the way, how's Gena?"

"How'd you know about Gena?"

"Sherlock knows all. Never underestimate my powers."

"I'll tell you one thing. She'd be prouder than you seem to be to have half ownership of Baby Savannah."

"I bet I know which half she'd like to own."

"You know, Friedman, Gena's a lot like you. You both want what you can't have."

On that fairly sobering note the conversation ended. I needed a fairly sobering note because I was getting so high that soon I was going to need Gepetto's ladder to scratch my ass. It was also mildly heartening to see that Stephanie had lost none of her acerbic wit. She had, for instance, a far better sense of humor than the cat. Of course, Stephanie and the other Village Irregulars were going to need all the sense of humor they could muster if they ever found out I'd written the note to Winnie. But graphology being such an inexact science, my little secret seemed pretty safe as I killed the lights, went to bed, and tried to sleep by counting Ratsos wearing pink tights and sleeveless "Re-elect Barney Frank" sweatshirts. It took a while getting to sleep using this method and besides being almost entirely ineffectual, it was a remarkably unpleasant experience. Perhaps, however, it was all for the best.

Not having heard a thing from upstairs all evening, I'd left the receiver in the "on" position. If I hadn't done that, or if I'd been sleeping more soundly, I never would've heard Winnie screaming.

21

I N the darkness the scream seemed to reverberate rather unpleasantly through the loft. I leaped sideways, threw on the bathrobe, and jumped into my armadillo slippers. By the digital clock on the bedside table it was only twelve forty-seven. Early to bed, early to rise, makes a man listen to a lesbian's cries. I was shuffling across the twilit living room wondering what the hell to do next, if anything, when the receiver crackled to life again.

"What are you doing here?" said a woman's voice, steeped in a frighteningly cold hysteria.

"So you're the dyke," said a stranger's voice, casual as a man on the street.

"Why are you wearing that?" said the woman.

"Where is she?" said the stranger.

The conversation sounded a bit like something you might hear on *The Young and the Restless* except that I wasn't very young and I wasn't very restless and I knew my receiver didn't pick up that channel. Besides, it was a little late in the day for the soaps. I was debating whether to call 911 or do a little housework and listen to some more, when the woman, whom I took to be Winnie, started screaming again, the guy started cursing, things started breaking, and I started dashing out the door and up the stairs.

If you've ever tried dashing up a rather dimly lit staircase in furry armadillo-shaped house slippers at one o'clock in the morning, you're probably aware that it can be a fairly daunting task. If I'd heard what I'd thought I'd heard over Rambam's device, my next task might be a hell of a lot tougher. By the time I'd gotten to Winnie's door, everything seemed as quiet as the tomb of the mummy of the Pharaoh Esophagus. I knocked on the door but there was no response. One of the things you don't much like to hear in this business is the sound of nothing. It usually means you're about to see something you're going to like even less.

The door was unlocked, so I opened it and walked in. The place was dark as Miller's Cave and there was a cold draft blowing in from somewhere. I called Winnie's name a few times but got no answer. The place was starting to give me a fairly tertiary case of the heebie-jeebies. I felt around on the wall for a light switch and after about two hours and forty-five minutes I found one and the loft lit up like a Christmas tree in Las Vegas.

Now there was lots of light on the subject but still no subject. Strangely enough, a clean, well-lighted place in which a crime has recently occurred can be spookier than anything Nancy Drew ever shined her flashlight on in the attic. Lesbian dance class lighting, apparently, was just about as bright as the burning bush, yet somewhere in the loft there lingered a redolent sense of dread and a feeling I can only describe as something very close to loneliness. Anytime you admit the possibility exists that you may soon be stumbling upon death, you will always find yourself alone no matter who's there. It's just one of life's little ways of letting you know your mother's not around to section your grapefruit anymore.

If there was a body, I didn't see it. If an assailant had been there, he'd fled and it wasn't too hard to guess his departure route. A window by the fire escape was gaping wide open like a horrible, accusatory mouth. For a brief, bewildering moment or two I wondered if the accusation could've been directed at myself. Had anything I'd done in my campaign of harassment against Winnie set the wheels in motion for whatever criminal action had occurred here? Was it even within the realm of conceivability that the attacker could've been one of the Village Irregulars? The voice on the receiver hadn't sounded familiar, but listening devices, according to Rambam, were endemic with distortions, much like everything else in the world.

The guilt swiftly passed as I once again began to appreciate the tenuous situation into which I'd propelled myself. I was a stranger like Camus, wearing fluffy armadillo-shaped house slippers, very possibly also like Camus, and now I found myself standing in a room where a crime had just taken place. Could the attacker have *entered* through the window and still be lurking about in some recess of the loft? Could he have abducted Winnie in the short time that had elapsed from the moment I heard her final screams to the present moment in which I unaccountably found myself both wishing I'd brought along a cigar and wondering what the hell I was going to do? Could a murderer right now be sitting at the kitchen table sipping Winnie's Red Zinger herbal tea with a sweet little serial killer's smile on his face and eyes that resembled carnival mirrors after the carnival's left town?

I thought again about calling 911, then I thought briefly of Sergeant Mort Cooperman and Sergeant Buddy Fox, then I figured death at the hands of a psycho was preferable and I might as well have a look around for myself. I was betting the guy had bugged out for the dugout and I hoped to God I was right because, short of kicking him to death with my armadillo slippers, it was going to be pretty unpleasant if I came face to face with him over what was left of the Gustav Stickley table.

I listened again for any telltale sounds, but there were none. All I could hear were the blurry half notes of the midnight machinery of the city penetrating the open window—almost like Allen Ginsberg humming a Buddhist prayer—then separating themselves from one another in my brain: sirens, car alarms, cash registers, human coke machines, elevators going down, the jumbled scripture of a junkie screaming through the veins of the subway, the ubiquitous ugly sound of rich people laughing, the two-legged rats rustling the garbage can timpani in the alley of the shadow of death; the cop is swinging his baton; the orchestra is tuning up.

I was looking for a victim or a perpetrator but no one was in the kitchen with Dinah. No one was in the dumper with her either. I checked all the closets as well, but, as I'd suspected, everybody'd come out of them a long time ago. That left only the bedroom.

I'd been in that bedroom before once in another lifetime when Winnie had thought she might possibly be heterosexual and I had thought I might possibly be king of the Gypsies. We'd both been wrong, of course, and now the place looked empty as a runway in *Casablanca*. But I only could glimpse that moment through the fog and the mystery of lesbianism. I didn't want to penetrate all the secrets of lesbianism any more than I wanted to see my bride before we walked down the aisle or see my baby actually being born. To want to know these secrets is the main reason modern man lacks the power and the magic of Davy Crockett, or Father Damien, or Peter Pan. I checked the bedroom closets. Zippo. I looked under the bed. No communists.

I walked back into the dance studio and thought about closing the window or calling the cops or going across the hallway and waking up Stephanie, but instead I wound up sitting on a sofa near a far wall and staring blankly at the brightly lit room like a late-night layover at La Guardia. For one thing, I was shivering either from the cold or from abject terror and I wanted to get that under control before I tried anything else.

There is an unnerving, unsettling feeling of violation when someone breaks into your home. Irrationally perhaps, I suddenly thought of the time I saw Siegfried and Roy in Las Vegas. Siegfried and Roy are two kraut tap dancers who make about half a million a night and spend all of it on face-lifts and the curiously Teutonic task of preserving a personal menagerie of rare white tigers while all the other remaining tigers on the planet are disappearing faster than a magic act. Recently, one of their rare white tigers mauled to death another one of their rare white tigers. Unfortunately, it did not maul to death Siegfried and Roy. The part of the show I liked best was when Roy is up on stage making his testicles disappear and suddenly Siegfried comes out of this hidden trapdoor in the middle of the audience and nearly jumps up your asshole and scares the hell out of everybody.

That was kind of like what happened to me as I sat there on Winnie's couch wondering what to do next. Suddenly, in a totally empty loft, I heard a ghostly voice very close by distinctly pronounce two words.

"Oh, shit," said the voice.

And, of course, I just about did.

22

WINNIE Katz was lying on the floor of the loft directly behind the large davenport upon which my buttocks were currently residing. If she hadn't muttered "Oh, shit," probably nobody would've found her in a million years. She did not, it should be noted, have a Man-In-Trouble Hotline arrangement like McGovern and myself. She was not even a man. She was, however, in trouble.

Winnie was starting to come around just as I started to come around the couch to where she was now sitting up on the floor holding her head. She registered my presence first with some mild surprise and then with her habitual expression of personal distaste, which I took as a healthy sign that she was probably going to live. People who love you always seem to die while people who hate your guts always seem to live forever. All you can do about it is to just go on being yourself and try not to get too involved.

"Winnie," I said, "who did this to you?"

"Fred Flintstone," she said.

"Are you okay? Is there anything I can do to help?"

"Yeah," said Winnie. "You can close that fucking window."

Actually, I thought, she looked and sounded just about normal. Somebody'd obviously given her a fairly good bonk on the head, of course. If she'd been a quarterback in the NFL you'd no doubt have wanted to take her out of the game. But she was a lot tougher than a quarterback; she was a lesbian dance instructor and she was damn well going to stay in the game if she wanted to. Even touching her could be dangerous to your health, education, and welfare. Lesbians are a sturdy breed, and that's mostly because they can't technically reproduce or replicate themselves and that also makes them a dying breed and they know this and that's why they don't want you to try to take them out of the game.

I walked over to the window in a state of some ambivalence. I'd expected to be feeling a little sorry for Winnie after the vicious attack she'd just experienced. Instead, I had to admit, I was beginning to feel the inklings of a grudging admiration. I looked out the window at the empty fire escape and the dark, empty street below. The garbage trucks had been the only witnesses, and they'd been sleeping.

I didn't close the window. I turned around to see Winnie standing in the lonely light of her violated studio, setting fire to a cigarette with a Zippo. The last time I'd been in the same room with her was years ago when I'd dropped the cat off on my way to Texas. At the time she'd been smoking Death Lite cigarettes, which she imported from London. Now, I noticed, she was smoking Players. My dear dead friend Tom Baker had once accused me of having a penchant for smoking off-brand cigarettes. Maybe Stephanie had been right. I was more like Winnie than I thought.

"You've come a long way, baby," I said. "Moving up from Death Lites to Players."

"It's a woman thing," she said. "Are you going to close that fucking window?"

"Well, I was thinking we might ought to call the cops. There might be fingerprints on the window and—"

"Fuck a bunch of fingerprints. There's no use in calling the cops. We'd probably freeze to death before they got here. Nice outfit, by the way."

"I'm glad you noticed," I said, as I stepped over and closed the window. "Why don't you tell me about this guy you call Fred Flintstone?"

"I wasn't making social commentary," she said. "He was wearing a Fred Flintstone mask."

Though I'd already closed the window, a slight, involuntary shiver went through me. It felt like little tiny suffragettes were marching up my spine. It didn't last long, but it lasted long enough. It left a sick afterimage in my mind. A guy wearing a Fred Flintstone mask attacking a lesbian. As Woody Allen's shrink often says: "What did he mean by that?"

"Did you notice anything else about the guy?"

"Yeah," said Winnie. "He had a gun in one hand and a knife in the other."

"C'mon, Winnie," I said, thinking maybe the guy'd hit her a little too hard. I'd never heard of an intruder carrying a gun in one hand and a knife in the other. Of course, most of them, I reflected, didn't wear Fred Flintstone masks either.

"If he had a gun and a knife," I said, "why in the hell do you think he didn't kill you?"

"Maybe he was trying to scare me."

"Did he?"

"Not as much as those house shoes."

Here was a woman, I thought, with pawnshop balls. As much as she may have irritated me in the past, and continued to get up my sleeve in the present, I had to admire her cool after such a traumatic event. There were not many women in this world, I figured, who would've been that cool, nor many men.

"By the way," said Winnie, "I didn't think I screamed *that* loud. How did you happen to hear me?"

"I was—uh—in the hallway."

"Not eavesdropping, I hope."

This was a little closer to home than I would've liked, but there was no way Winnie could've known we'd bugged her loft. I was trying to think of a good reason for my having been out in the hallway at one in the morning and all I could think of was that the cat was probably listening to our whole conversation right now and enjoying the fact that I appeared to have gotten my tail in a bit of a crack.

"Of course not," I said indignantly. "I was in the hallway taking out the cat litter. I dump the cat litter every seven years whether I need to or not. Now, tell me, did this guy happen to say anything to you?"

"Yeah," said Winnie. "Just before he hit me with the gun he said something, but I'm not sure what it was."

"Think," I said. "Cast your mind back. This could be important."

"Oh yeah, I remember," said Winnie. "The last thing he said was 'See you around.'"

"'See you around'?"

"He said it in a casual, almost friendly way. In fact, that scared me more than the gun or the knife."

I asked Winnie again if she was all right, if she wanted me to stay, if she wanted me to call somebody to come over to keep her company, and she said yes, no, and no, and I could see that she meant it. I told her to call me immediately if there was any sign of the guy returning or if she needed anything at all or just wanted to talk. Then I almost hugged her but settled for patting her on the shoulder in the way a man might demonstrate to another man that he's proud of him. Then I got the hell out of there.

My door was wide open when I walked back into the loft and I was feeling a little unhinged myself. The cat was sitting on the desk looking at me expectantly. I fetched a cigar out of Sherlock's head, cut the end off with my butt-cutter, and fired that booger up. Then I poured a stiff shot of snakepiss into the bull's horn and poured the whole thing rapidly down my neck. My uvula wasn't real happy about the experience, but the rest of me started feeling a tad better. The cat was still staring at me intently.

Either because the cat willed it or because I was turning into a walking web of deception, I decided to validate one of my statements to Winnie. I would take out the cat litter. I would dump it neatly into the nearby Dumpster, where one of the nearby garbage trucks would probably pick it up about the time I saw my next Siegfried and Roy show. A bit of the litter spilled out in the hallway as I was navigating the dimly lit staircase, but it didn't bother me. I believed in recycling. After all, some of the dried cat turds had been around for quite a while and could've been carbon-dated, very possibly, back to Ed Meese's childhood. In another million years one of them could be the fucking Hope Diamond. Obviously, somebody else believed in recycling, too.

As I dumped the cat litter I looked up at the windows of Winnie's flat. The lights were still on up there and I didn't blame her. When a guy in a Fred Flintstone mask with a gun in one hand and a knife in the other says, "See you around," it means that sooner or later you almost definitely will. I thought of my childish threat note to Winnie and my Merry Prankster–style campaign of mischief against her. Thus does life imitate artifice, I thought to myself.

"Do you know that old Bee Gees song?" I said to the cat as I returned to the loft. " 'I Started a Joke'?"

The cat did not respond in any manner that could possibly be construed as even the barest attempt at communication. Her eyes were wide, unblinking, unthinking whirlpools of wisdom she preferred to keep completely to herself. You couldn't really fault her on that one, however. The Bee Gees were way before her time.

23

WHEN I woke up in the morning I couldn't believe my ears. I'd been having a not unpleasant dream about a small, freckle-faced, Norman Rockwell–type child counting out loud as he pulled the legs off the Dancing Itos, and before I could even leap sideways I heard Winnie Katz's strident voice counting out loud in my loft.

"At the bar," she said. "Five, six, seven, eight!"

Then the music started, always accompanied, of course, by irritating shuffling and thumping noises. Before I'd gotten halfway to the espresso machine, Winnie was shrieking like a Fury to be heard over the music.

"Lines of five across the floor! Use your *center!*"

"Unpleasant," I said to the cat.

The cat, of course, said nothing, though she did appear to gaze upward with some concern when a small piece of plaster dropped like dandruff from God directly between the two empty workmen's ladders. Vinnie and Gepetto, it should be noted, had taken to arriving for work at increasingly later hours. Pretty soon, I suspected, they'd be calling it in from the Italian deli down the street. You really couldn't blame them, of course. The ceiling seemed to be falling faster than they could plaster.

When I finally got the espresso machine up and running, it, too, chimed in with the dance music, humming something that sounded suspiciously like a tinny Italian version of "The Little Drummer Boy." Penetrating this cacophony, at moments when you least suspected, came Winnie's piercing commands, exhorting her pupils to an ever higher degree of excellence.

"Keep your tailbone curved under!" she shouted above the din.

"Words to live by," I said to the cat.

I was clearly of two minds, I reflected, as I stood idly by the kitchen window watching a pigeon shit on a parked garbage truck. Unfortunately, both of those minds were starting to cook on another planet. Part of me was being driven to distraction by the ongoing activities upstairs and did not feel one shard of regret about encouraging my small band of Watsons to worm their way into Winnie's world. The other part of me was still somewhat shaken by the events of the previous night. The situation, which started as a mere prank, had now become an actual real-life-and-death scenario for the victim of my prank, Winnie Katz. It was not my fault that somebody wearing a Fred Flintstone mask had attacked and threatened her. Nonetheless, possibly because of the awkward timing of my bogus threat note, I felt vaguely remorseful. Was it conceivable, now that all my Watsons were in place, that they could do what God and Arthur Conan Doyle had intended and help me catch the true culprit? Highly unlikely, I thought, as I briefly reflected upon the misguided talents of the Village Irregulars. And yet one never knew. Watson was loyal. Watson was persistent. Watson was ubiquitous. Maybe that was enough.

It was a dangerous idea, I thought, as I drew a hot cup of espresso from the machine and resurrected a half-smoked dead soldier with a kitchen match. It could put the Village Irregulars in danger not to mention placing Winnie in more danger than she was already in if that were possible. I could, of course, concoct a reason to pull the Village Irregulars off this increasingly risky assignment. But, as I listened to the incessant racket overhead, the first part of me didn't want to do that yet. Besides, once you've wound a Watson up and turned him loose, it isn't the easiest thing to get him back to Baker Street to listen to Sherlock saw a violin.

"This is *not* a dance step you can learn!" Winnie's voice screamed through the receiver. "I call this the Kinesthetic Delight! Move your body however it wants to be moved!"

This was getting me nowhere I wanted to be very quickly. I switched off the receiver, picked up the blower on the left, and called Rambam. In fairly short order, I told him what had happened last night and gave him Winnie's account of the attack and the gunman.

"The Fred Flintstone mask I can deal with," I said, "but the knife in one hand and the gun in the other sounds crazy to me."

"Wrong," said Rambam. "Carrying both a knife and a gun has become very trendy these days. You use the gun to get the victim either tied up or positioned properly. Then you use the knife to croak him. For one thing, it's much quieter. For another, you don't get blood all over your clothes like you would if you tried to stab a struggling victim."

"I can see the advantages."

"Why the mask though? Did she know this character?"

"She's not sure. He *was* wearing a mask."

"Obviously, he thinks she might know him. He sounds crazy enough to have written that note, too. I've got the graphologist working on it, by the way."

"That's good."

"You don't sound too excited."

"Well, it *is* an inexact science."

"So's killing somebody."

"That's true, but—"

"The one thing I'm pretty sure of is that the guy means business. He was just playing with her this time. I think he'll be back soon to finish the job."

"So what should I do?"

"You could call the police."

"She doesn't want me to do that."

"You could dress up as a dinosaur and wait out on the fire escape and if he shows up in a Fred Flintstone mask again you could eat him. How the hell do I know what you should do? I'm leaving this afternoon to chase Nazis in Canada with my friend Joey Schacter. I've found over two hundred of the bastards that the government didn't even know were there."

"How'd you find them?"

"The fucking telephone book. The bastards never even bothered to change their names. And get this. The Nazis are beating the hell out of the actuarial tables. Only a few are in the hospital and only two of my group have croaked. They seem to live forever."

"One more example of the good guys dying and the bad guys living happily ever after. Why do you think that is?"

"My theory is they're afraid to die."

"So am I. If you're going to be out of touch for a while, it could get ugly here. Now c'mon, what am I supposed to do?"

"I told you. Dress up like a dinosaur. As long as you don't go around in Ratso drag it's okay with me. Look, it's just as likely the guy won't be back. So don't worry about it. How's the bug working, by the way?"

"A little too well. I'm getting tired of hearing Winnie shouting: 'Keep your tailbone curved under!' "

"That's the best advice I've heard for both of us," said Rambam.

The thought of Rambam being away for a while was a bit unsettling to me, and so was everything else. So when I cradled the blower I decided to get out of the loft for a bit and maybe drown my troubles in some wonton soup at Big Wong's *sans* Ratso. I didn't know if Vinnie and Gepetto were coming back at all or if the guy with the Fred Flintstone mask was coming back, but I figured the first one back could let the other ones in. I got dressed, grabbed a few cigars for the road, and headed for the door. I left the cat in charge.

At Big Wong's all the waiters kept asking me, "Where Ratso?" I told them, "He turned gay." They all laughed and said, "Chee-Chee! Chee-Chee!" This, indeed, lent some degree of credence to the theory that they believed Ratso and I were homosexual lovers. What Chinese waiters, lesbian dancers, Nazis in Canada, or anybody else might think should never bother you too much. It is, however, just another good reason to keep your tail-bone curved under.

24

SOMETIMES the best way to handle a tedious situation is to leave it alone. It's never worked for me, but that didn't stop me from trying it again. Clearly, a diversion was needed to get me away from the loft for a while and away from the out-of-control forces that, I had to admit, had been set into play to a large part by myself. A challenging hobby for me, I felt, might be to pursue the matter of Joe the Hyena's daughter. With Rambam busy chasing Nazis in Canada, of course, I'd be pretty much left to my own devices. But Rambam was not the only consultant private investigator in my stable. Kent Perkins was a PI in L.A., a longtime friend of mine, and one who'd helped me on several crucial cases, including the singularly dangerous adventure of finding Ratso's true birth mother. Kent also had something going for him that Rambam didn't have. He was married to Ruth Buzzi. Ruth Buzzi was as Italian as you could get. After twenty years of his marriage to Ruth, I figured, maybe some of it had rubbed off.

Vinnie and Gepetto had knocked off early, which was just as well when you're trying to pick up leads on Joe the Hyena's deceased daughter. A lot appeared to be going on upstairs, from the sounds filtering down from the roof. Maybe Brennan and McGovern were killing each other. Maybe Gena was successfully seducing Stephanie. Maybe a large number of lesbians were simply moving their bodies the way they wanted to be moved. Possibly out of respect to Winnie, after the ugly attack of the previous night, I decided to keep the receiver turned off for a while. Besides, the various Village Irregulars would no doubt be reporting in later that night. I lit up a Cuban Montecristo #2 cigar and began my search for the woman Joe the Hyena and I agreed I had rescued from a mugger in a bank. The espresso machine was living proof that Joe believed I'd saved his daughter. Then why had Vinnie so vehemently insisted that Joe didn't have a daughter and then later amended that information with the fact that Joe *had* had a daughter but that she'd died three years before I claimed to have saved her from the mugger? Certainly Vinnie might've told me that Joe had no daughter before he'd gotten to know me, then, when he got to trust me a bit more, he'd given me a more complete picture. Vinnie, of all people, would know that you don't spread false personal rumors about your employer, especially if your employer is Joe the Hyena.

"This little puzzle is complicated," I said to the cat, "by the fact that you can't just pick up the blower and ask Joe the Hyena how I could've rescued his daughter if she'd died three years earlier? If I did something like that I could wind up with a garbage truck in my bed."

The cat, of course, said nothing, which, considering the subject matter, might've been the smartest thing to do. I took a few preparatory puffs on the cigar, and then I called Kent Perkins's number in Los Angeles.

"Allied Management," came the secretary's voice on the blower. She sounded like a happy little California person.

"Kent Perkins, please," I said. "Tell him his favorite Texas Jewboy is calling from New York."

"I'll need your name, sir," said the secretary in a slightly more officious tone.

"Richard Kinky 'Big Dick' Friedman."

"Is this an emergency?" she asked rather curtly.

"Not yet."

I winked at the cat and waited. In a few moments Kent's friendly Texas drawl crawled out of the blower and into my consciousness.

"Hey, Big Dick," said Kent. "I'm glad to see you haven't lost your touch. You seem to have terribly agitated my secretary."

"Was she terribly agitated about the Texas Jewboy part or the Big Dick part?"

"I'll ask her when she stops hyperventilating. You know I've got my own private investigation firm now. Twenty-seven employees."

"Jesus," I said. "You've moved up from a friend to a contact. Look, Kent, I'll get to the meat of it. I just need a little professional direction. I'm trying to locate a woman who died three years before I met her."

"Sounds like my first wife," said Kent.

I filled Kent in on as much as he needed to know. Like a good little private investigator, he had a few questions.

"Why don't you talk to your friend Rambam about this? It's right up his alley."

"Because he's in Canada chasing Nazis."

"I never knew there were Nazis in Canada."

"Yes, Virginia, there are Nazis in Canada. Now are you going to get off your ass and help me find out about this damn dead broad or not?"

"You sweet-talker, you. What's Joe the Hyena's real name?"

"I don't know."

"What was his daughter's name?"

"I don't know."

"Well, it's a start. Okay, here's what you could do. I don't say you should—but you could. Find some Italians in the know and get Joe the Hyena's real name. If he's some heavy mobster, it shouldn't be too hard to find out. If you're still alive after that, you could check with city hall about the death certificate for the daughter. Of course, if she didn't die there, it won't be there. So that really hasn't helped you much."

"Neither have you."

"Now what could've upset my secretary? Okay, Kink, here's a better plan. In fact, it just might work. Find the Catholic hospitals in Brooklyn—you know, Our Lady of the East River—names like that, and check out her birth certificate."

"I'm trying to find out if she's *dead,* Inspector Clouseau. Why would I want her *birth* certificate?"

"Because these mob guys are pretty much all hard-core Catholics. They may kill forty-seven guys but they think if they say enough Hail Marys and have enough money they can pave their way to salvation. I think they sprinkle a little holy water on the kid on the third day or something. Whatever it is, it's a lot kinder than what you guys do. I wouldn't know, of course, being a good ol' Southern Baptist myself."

"Like I always say, the only thing wrong with Southern Baptists is they don't hold them under long enough. What the hell's the point of all this?"

"The point is that most of these religious mob families retain the same priest or monsignor for their entire lives. His name should be on the birth certificate. Find the priest and you'll find the answer to your little riddle."

"Perkins," I said, "that's brilliant."

"Now there'll be a lot of nuns around these hospitals probably. You might want to go out and buy yourself a big ol' cross to wear. You won't get very far if they find out you're a Jeeeeeewww!"

In a vain effort to irritate me, Kent often pronounced the word "Jew," like many Texans, employing about eleven syllables.

Ironically, when a Texan says the word "Jewish," it's spoken invariably with only one syllable. But I was far too excited to be irritated. This was going to be good therapy for me to get involved with an interesting little puzzle that had nothing whatever to do with the lesbian circus upstairs. Not only that, but I'd be doing it without Rambam or the Village Irregulars.

"Thanks, Kent," I said. "This is great. I'll probably have this thing solved before Rambam even gets back."

"Is he really hunting Nazis in Canada?"

"That's an affirmative."

"Why doesn't he hunt them here in the U.S.?"

"Too easy," I said.

25

THE cat adored Vinnie. I suppose he was a more active presence in the loft now that I was becoming more absorbed in what I saw as the intellectual exercise of finding out exactly whom I rescued in the bank ten years ago. The woman had refused to file charges against the mugger, deciding not even to hang around until the police arrived. All I remembered was a slim, attractive, auburn-haired young woman telling me "Thanks" with tears in her eyes and then walking across Seventh Avenue and disappearing somewhere into Sheridan Square. There had been rumors, but only rumors, that the woman had been Kathy Smith, the Canadian girl who'd been with John Belushi when he'd died. These were never substantiated and anyway, I had come, I must admit, to like the idea that I'd saved Joe the Hyena's daughter. If Vinnie was correct and she'd already been dead by that time, then Joe was mistaken, I was mistaken, and the espresso machine was an illegitimate child. But I dared not discuss the matter any further with Vinnie. There was no doubt where his loyalties resided. If he thought I was snooping around in this old, long-dead business, in the words of Rambam, he'd rat me out in a heartbeat. But I never mentioned any of this to the cat, of course. The cat adored Vinnie.

"You know," said that object of the cat's affection, "dis puppet head don't look too happy sittin' on top of dis dusty old refrigerator."

"What're you talking about?" I said, joining Vinnie by the refrigerator. "That's one of the friendliest smiles in New York."

"Yeah, it's friendly all right," said Vinnie. "But look at him close. Can't you see he's fakin' it?"

I looked closely at the puppet head. Then I looked closely at Vinnie. Was he another candidate for life on the installment plan at Dr. Gachet's bed and breakfast? I didn't know if he was crazy or just had a whimsical, sensitive streak you never seem to notice when a guy is standing on a ladder, plastering a ceiling.

"Maybe you're right," I said. "But what can we do about it?"

"He don't want to be on top a dat refrigerator. He wants to be sitting on a nice mantelpiece over a nice warm fireplace. We could build it for him."

"That'd be great," I said, "but I can't afford it."

"Let me make a phone call," said Vinnie.

I nodded, and Vinnie walked over to the desk, picked up the blower, and dialed a number. The conversation was distinguished only by the fact that Vinnie used no names, numbers or addresses. In his line of work, I thought, you had to be careful these days. You never knew if somebody else was listening. Nonetheless, it wasn't difficult to figure out to whom he was speaking.

"It's me," said Vinnie.

The cat sat nearby on the desk.

"Is he there?"

I looked out the window and pretended I wasn't home.

"Can you put him on?"

A garbage truck moved on Vandam Street.

"Yeah, it's me. I'm at the guy's place with the ceiling."

I looked up at the ceiling. It was still hanging in there.

"Right. We're thinkin' of puttin' in a fireplace. What do you think?"

The cat looked at me, then at Vinnie. I looked back out the window. The garbage truck had stopped.

"Yeah, I'll tell him. *Ciao.*"

Vinnie hung up the phone and clapped his hands together, momentarily startling the cat. The cat, the puppet head, and myself all stared eagerly in his direction.

"Looks like you got yourself a fireplace," said Vinnie.

"Great," I said. "But aren't there things like building codes to consider?"

"Who do you think writes the building codes?" said Vinnie. "By the way, the fireplace is on Joe."

"That's terrific."

"But the ceiling's on you."

"I hope you don't mean literally," I said.

With Vinnie and Gepetto around I kept the receiver off most of the time, but when I occasionally turned it on and voices came across, they did not seem particularly curious. Maybe they thought I was a ham operator or a mad scientist or something. Aside from hearing Winnie's encounter with Fred Flintstone, the phyzagometer device hadn't been quite as helpful a tool as I'd expected. Once the novelty and the vicarious excitement had worn off, which had taken about two minutes, all the dingus had really provided me was a stereo soundtrack for what I was already hearing through the ceiling. Of course, I had heard Ratso's speech to the lesbians and Gena's attempted seduction of Stephanie, but in general the programing was pretty weak, not the kind of thing that kept me or the cat riveted to the receiver, not the kind of thing that would help me find Fred Flintstone. It should be noted as well that Winnie had not asked for my help in this matter and when I'd offered it, she'd declined my offer. Nevertheless, I thought with a grim smile, I'd helped her anyway. I'd sent her the Village Irregulars.

Regardless of Rambam's warning, I didn't feel that Winnie, the girls, or my crew of troublemakers were in any immediate danger. When they checked in with me I'd simply tell them that there'd been another incident the previous night, an attack upon Winnie, and so if they see a masked man running around on the fire escape with a gun in one hand and a knife in the other, Halloween's over and it's each man for himself.

After Vinnie and Gepetto, having taken elaborate fireplace measurements, had left for the day, I put the zoo and a half that currently occupied the loft above me out of my mind and thought about my old friend and former road manager Sal Lorello, who lived in Chappaqua. Sal was Italian and he'd had his hip card punched. Maybe he could help me with the Hyena situation.

"Hey, Kinky man," said Sal when he answered the phone. "What's happenin'? You ready to go back out on the road?"

This was a little joke of Sal's. Our years on the road together had almost killed him and they hadn't exactly been brick and mortar to my well-being either.

"I was ready yesterday," I said.

"Forget it," said Sal. "Keep your day job. I keep hearing stories about all the cases you've solved and all the bad guys you've caught. I'd stay with that. It's a lot safer than being a country singer."

"You read my mail, Sal. That's what I was calling you about. I'm working on a little investigation right now and I think maybe you can help me."

"Proud to be of service," said Sal. "What do you need?"

"I need to find the real name of this Italian guy. I only know the name people call him."

"What do people call him?"

"Joe the Hyena."

There was a silence on the line that sounded like the end of the world. I plucked a fresh Cuban cigar out of Sherlock's head, went through all the prenuptials and preignition procedures and still the silence held.

"Sal?"

"Huh?"

"I thought you passed away."

"That's what I'm worried about."

"C'mon, Sal, the guy's not Al Capone. All I'm asking for is somebody's last name."

"And all I'm telling you is you didn't hear it from me. *Capisce?*"

"Jesus, Sal, this isn't a rerun of *The Untouchables*. It's your old pal the Kinkster asking you for some guy's name. How hard is that?"

"Look, I don't know his name. I don't even want to know his name. But I know somebody who does. I'll ask him and I'll call you back."

"Don't take too long. I don't want to wake up tomorrow morning with a horse's ass in my bed."

"Beats visiting the fish," said Sal.

When you live in a world you tend to get caught up in it. For most of us, cops and robbers is just a game for kids. But Italians growing up in the city can get pretty touchy, pretty nervous, and sometimes a stiff sidecar of both. That's why it's always good to be a Jew in New York. You know cops and robbers is just a game, so you spread your bets around, buy season tickets, and never fully appreciate the fact that Jewish and Italian grandmothers are all five feet tall and five feet wide and completely interchangeable.

Two hours later, Sal called me from a pay phone. By this time, I was getting kind of nervous about the situation myself. Once again, he swore me to secrecy.

"You didn't hear this from me," said Sal.

146

"Of course not."

"You didn't even get this phone call."

"Of course not."

"We never even talked about it."

"Of course not."

"I'll say one word. *Capisce?*"

"The guy's name is Capisce?"

"Of course not," said Sal.

"Then, for God's sake, Sal, what the hell's the name?"

"Tortellini," he said.

26

SOMEWHERE around nine bells I turned the receiver back on and listened to Winnie and the girls exchange their fond farewells as well as exchanging a few phone numbers and hobbies. There was a rather sensuous-sounding lesbian locker-room ambience up there that led one to suspect a lot more than mere dancing was occurring. Many of the girls, apparently, had taken Winnie's words to heart. From the sound of things, they seemed to be moving their bodies the way they wanted to be moved.

As I listened rather distractedly to the receiver, I began the somewhat laborious experience of checking out Catholic hospitals in Brooklyn. I'd suspected there would not be many. I'd suspected that Catholic hospitals in Brooklyn would be like Polish war heroes or black yachtsmen I had known. I'd suspected wrong. There were lots of other Our Ladies besides Our Lady of the East River. There were so many Our Ladies, in fact, that I started to feel like a rising young urologist in a singles bar. In which hospital had Joe Tortellini's daughter, whom I liked to think of as Baby Hyena, been born? Was it Our Lady of the

Baseball Bat? Our Lady of the Tire Iron? Our Lady of the Meathook?

"So many ladies," I said to the cat, "so little time."

The cat, of course, said nothing. She was not a Catholic. Too much dogma.

"By my rough assessment," I continued, "Baby Hyena appeared to be in her early twenties when I rescued her in the bank on Christopher Street. That was approximately ten years ago. That means the Our Lady we're looking for has to be at least thirty years old."

It wasn't that old for a lady, I reflected, as I made a few notes in my Big Chief tablet, but it certainly eliminated a lot of hospitals. As the possibility of actually solving my little puzzle grew increasingly feasible, so I grew increasingly engrossed in the project. If nothing else, it might clear up a bit of unexplained trivia from days gone by, not to mention providing me a chance to polish up my somewhat rusty investigative chops. Besides, if you find you've got too many lesbians in your life, it's always a nice change of pace to go out and meet some nuns.

Suddenly, there came two almost simultaneous sets of knocking upon my chamber door. One set appeared to be somewhere near the top of the door and the other, somewhere quite a bit closer to the floor. Both knockers appeared to be highly agitato.

"MIT . . . MIT . . . MIT!" shouted one voice I couldn't help recognizing. "Kink! Kink! Open up!"

"Better let us in, mate," chimed in the other voice. "McGovern's got us all in a rather bloody sticky wicket!"

"Fuck you, Brennan," said McGovern. "At least I didn't piss in the sink."

"That's because we don't have a bloody pot to piss in," said Brennan, "now that you've blown the whole sodding investigation!"

"I blew the investigation? Winnie loves *me*."

"Winnie could care less if you were hanging by the balls from the ballet bar, mate. Winnie loves being written up in the *Times* of London."

"Maybe I *will* write her up in the *Times* of London."

"Maybe I'll slit my penis like an aboriginal and fly to the bloody moon!"

"Who's there?" I said in a rather futile effort to leaven the tension convention at my doorstep.

"Open the bloody door, mate, before I kill McGovern," said Brennan.

"I'd like to fucking see that one," said McGovern, his loud, infectious Irish laughter raising the decibel level even higher in the hallway.

I opened the door and ushered the two erstwhile friends into the loft. I aimed both of them at my meager liquor supply while I reclaimed my cigar from the Texas-shaped ashtray on my desk. Then I aimed myself toward the kitchen counter and joined them.

"There seems to be a bit of rancor in the ranks, gentlemen," I said, pouring all of us stiff shots of Jameson's. "Suppose someone informs me as to what's going on in Winnie World."

"Someone's been making crank calls to Winnie's studio all day," said McGovern. "We think it's the same sick fuck who wrote the note."

"That was no reason for you to tell her about the note, mate," said Mick Brennan.

"Well, here's to old friends," I said, holding up the bull's horn to toast the two of them. Somewhat grudgingly, they raised their shot glasses. Then we killed the shots and things seemed to settle down a bit for the moment.

"Where's Winnie now?" I asked. "And how's her current mental health?"

"She's gone out somewhere with that Stephanie bird from across the hall," said Mick. "She's really upset, mate."

"That's understandable," I said. "An intruder broke in last

night with a gun and a knife and a Fred Flintstone mask, shook her up pretty good, said he'd see her around, then conked her on the head. Didn't she tell you guys about it?"

"No," said McGovern, "but that's probably the same guy who wrote the note and made the crank calls. Mick took one of them himself."

"Right," said Mick. "The guy calls and I pick up the phone and all he says in a bloody nasty tone of voice is, 'Where's the dyke?' So I says to him, 'Which one, mate?' and he hangs up."

"I've grown kind of fond of Winnie," said McGovern. "I wouldn't want to see anybody causing her any kind of grief. And I didn't tell her about the note. I merely asked her about it."

"Tell him what she answered, mate," said Brennan.

"She totally denies she ever received it," said McGovern.

"A classic case of subconscious blocking," I said, puffing confidently upon my Freudian cigar. I poured us all a generous second round. We all poured the generous second round down our necks.

"Speaking of subconscious blocking," said McGovern, "quite unintentionally, we did pick up another little piece of information. I'm not certain exactly how it impacts upon the investigation."

"Spit it," I said.

"Ratso swings both ways," said McGovern.

"I've heard rumors to that effect," I said, winking to the cat.

The cat looked on rather disdainfully, then turned her attention to a cockroach climbing the far wall. She was ready to believe anything anyone said about Ratso.

"Well," said Brennan, "now you have confirmation. He's a poofter, mate."

"We all have our human frailties, Mick—"

"That's true," said Brennan. "Especially McGovern."

"Don't start in on me now, you toxic little bastard," said McGovern.

"Maybe if we tried a little harder to understand Ratso," I said. "Maybe if we reached out a bit more, I think—"

"I don't care what you think, mate," said Brennan. "I'm not going to lay my dick on his bloody wisdom tooth."

"That's a bit homophobic," said McGovern, "for a guy who's been photographing as well as *ogling* a lesbian dance class for the past two days—"

"*I'm* ogling the bloody dance class?" said Brennan. "At least I keep my bloody hands on my tripod."

"I keep my hands on my tripod, too," said McGovern.

"Gentlemen, gentlemen, gentlemen," I said. "Sexual proclivities aside, we must tread very cautiously now. There is an extremely dangerous psycho out there, whose identity and motivations we have yet to learn, who is threatening Winnie Katz's life and very possibly placing our own lives in some jeopardy. We must be on the alert at all times, because in all likelihood, he will soon return to make good on his threats."

At precisely that moment, there came a startlingly loud banging on the door, which just about caused my cigar to fall from my mouth into the third round of Jameson's I was pouring. A loud voice carried clearly to all of us from out in the hallway.

"Kinkstah!" it said. "Open up, baby! I've got some big news, Kinkstah!"

There was no way around it. I walked over to the door and let Ratso into the loft. He came in wearing his standard coonskin cap, pink ostrich cowboy boots, phlegm-colored corduroy pants, and some kind of gold lamé cape that made him look like a gay matador. He was carrying a very small, rather effeminate-looking suitcase.

"What you got in the suitcase?" asked Brennan somewhat guardedly.

"Gym clothes," said Ratso.

"So what's the big news?" asked McGovern.

"Oh," said Ratso, looking around rather uncomfortably, "it'll keep."

I filled Ratso in on the Fred Flintstone situation. Then, as sort of a salesman's icebreaker, I was preparing to offer him a drink, always providing, of course, that there was anything left to drink. McGovern and Brennan had been surreptitiously slipping in a few rounds of their own. You know how it is when old friends get together. I was looking in the cabinet for another bottle of anything that was younger than I was, when a terrible din erupted that sounded very much like the world was coming to an end. Personally, I didn't care if the world came to an end just as long as it took me with it. And the Village Irregulars, of course. And the cat, it goes without saying.

At first I thought the roof was finally caving in, but I looked up and it seemed to still be there. Then I thought, quite irrationally, that McGovern was somehow upstairs rapidly sitting on various large pieces of furniture one after another and sending them crashing to the floor with his great, daunting, white, luminous buttocks. But McGovern was standing in my kitchen staring in the direction of the phyzagometer-receiver setup on my desk. Between the noise filtering down through the ceiling and the much louder squawkings emanating from the receiver, it sounded like Jerry Lewis was going down on the *Titanic* inside your head.

"What," said McGovern, pointing an accusatory finger at the bugging device, "is that?"

Ratso and Brennan, I noticed, seemed to be focusing their attention in the same direction as McGovern. In our technologically driven society, they all seemed to be more taken aback by the knowledge that I'd been bugging Winnie's loft than by whatever was currently happening up there. The great crashing noises continued at periodic intervals while the three of them, with the cat now joining in, maintained doubtful, questioning stares at the Kinkster. Even as several small pieces of plaster fell from the ceiling, the combined gaze of my comrades remained unwavering. The one thing I hadn't figured on happening, apparently, had happened. The Village Irregulars, with their own peculiar moralities, appeared to have bonded with Winnie Katz.

"I can explain," I said.

27

AND, of course, I could've explained. I could've simply told them what was a fairly close approximation of the truth. A dangerously deranged individual was stalking Winnie, and since she wasn't cooperating with the investigation, I was forced to bug her dance studio for her personal protection. My original motivation in the matter, or the fact that I'd written the threatening note myself, was none of their beeswax, cornbread, or shoe tacks. Anyway, I'd changed my mind about Winnie lately. It was no longer clear who was fooling whom and it almost didn't matter anymore. A gun, a knife, and a Fred Flintstone mask will sometimes do that to you. As things transpired, however, I never got to explain a damn thing to the little group gathered around me. A voice barely dancing on the edge of sanity could now be heard screeching through the receiver.

"Where are you, bitch?" he screamed. "Where are you?"

"That's our boy, mate," said Brennan. "That's the same voice I heard on the phone today."

"Sounds like Othello with a New York accent," said McGovern, as we all gathered closer to the receiver.

"Your father can't save you! Nobody can save you!" ranted the madman upstairs. "If I can't have you, nobody can!"

"That's not Othello," said Ratso. "It's O.J."

"Same difference, mate," said Brennan.

"Not quite," I said. "Othello had more class."

"Let's do something about him," said McGovern. "Call the cops."

"By the time they get here," said Ratso, "he could be in Chicago."

"That's true, mate," said Brennan. "I think it's up to us."

"There *are* four of us," said McGovern.

"We don't have a bloody gun in one hand and a bloody knife in the other," said Brennan.

"We've got to do something," said Ratso. "We can't just let him get away."

"You're right," I said.

"If we approached him," said McGovern, "we'd have to be very careful."

"You're right," I said.

"If we approached him," said Brennan, "we'd have to be very stupid."

"You're right, too," I said.

As Fred Flintstone continued his chilling soliloquy, I made a fateful decision. If we let him get away this time, next time might be too late. I went over to the corner by the refrigerator and came back with my dusty old Louisville Slugger baseball bat.

"Grab your weapons, gentlemen," I shouted. "The game is afoot."

The cat watched us all in wonder, possibly to see just how crazy we were. Ratso walked over to the sink and grabbed a kitchen knife. Brennan lifted his aforementioned tripod over his head. McGovern stared somewhat dubiously at the three of us, then grabbed from the counter the empty Jameson's bottle.

"Okay," I said, as we gathered by the doorway of the loft, "just be alert and be careful. The simultaneous carrying of a gun and a knife is not uncommon these days, according to Rambam. He says it's the mark of a pro."

"Great," said Ratso, "where the hell's Rambam now?"

"Chasing Nazis in Canada," I said.

"Some guys'll do anything," said McGovern, "to avoid a dangerous assignment."

The receiver had suddenly gone silent. If Fred Flintstone hadn't already fled, he would very soon, I suspected. If we were to have any hope of trapping him in Winnie's loft, we had to move now.

"Ratso," I said, "you'll come with me. We'll go up the stairs and in the front door. McGovern, you and Mick go out the kitchen window and up the fire escape. But watch it. That's how he got away last time."

"Thanks for the tip, pal," said McGovern.

"Okay," I said, "let's move!"

A SWAT team's a SWAT team, even if its members have never swatted a fly. The crouching stance is there instinctively and so's the choreography. I don't know if it's because as children in America we'd watched a lot of television, or because as adults in America we were cognizant of the imminent approach of a deadly reckoning. For whatever reason, as Ratso and I flung open the door and ran SWAT-like up the stairway, I clutched the baseball bat with the strength and intensity of a drowning witch.

Out of the blue, I recalled a recent conversation I'd had with Vinnie about the baseball bat. At the time, it hadn't seemed like anything with which I'd ever encounter hands-on experience.

"Dese wooden bats are da best," he'd said.

"You don't like the metal ones?"

"Dere da woist. You can do more damage to yourself wit dem when you bounce off something."

"Something like what?"

"Heads, arms, legs mostly. Now you can really hurt yourself hitting somebody's head or leg with a metal bat. A wooden bat cushions the blow. You hit 'em in the head just right you can hear it go 'squish.'"

"You've actually done this?"

"Only about two hundred times. Using da wooden bat, of course. Hey, I'm only kiddin'."

But I didn't think Vinnie had been kidding. And I knew Fred Flintstone wasn't kidding. That was fine. I wasn't kidding anymore either.

The fifth-floor hallway was about as bright and cheery as a coal mine in South Africa. Ratso and I slipped up to the door of Winnie's studio and I gently turned the knob. Unlike the previous night, the door was locked.

"What do we do now, Kinkstah?" said Ratso from behind me in a stage whisper that almost made me drop the baseball bat.

"We could knock and shout, 'Let us in! Let us in!' Then he'd probably come to the door and say, 'Not by the hair of my chinny-chin-chin.' Then McGovern could sneak up behind him and hit him with the bottle of Jameson's."

"What if he opens the door holding a gun and a knife?"

"You *can't* open a door holding a gun and a knife, Ratso."

"So what do we do?"

"Well, McGovern and Brennan have had ample time to seal off the fire-escape exit. I say we pretend we're the police."

Ratso nodded his agreement, and that's what we did. We banged loudly on the door and shouted, "Open up! Police!" in what we hoped were deep, gruff, convincing voices with just the slightly bored hint of another-day-at-the-office. Ratso held the knife in front of him like a character in *West Side Story* and I squeezed the bat even tighter, determined to make a squish sound upon the head of whoever opened that door. Fortunately, perhaps, nobody did.

We were getting tired of alternating the phrases "Open up! Police!" with "Police! Open the door!" when I thought I heard some movement inside the loft. I signaled to Ratso and we both pulled our lips together and leaned close to the door to listen. Footsteps were definitely coming toward the door.

"Hold your fire," said a voice I didn't recognize. "I'm coming."

As the door opened, Ratso and I burst in upon a large man holding both of his hands over his head. The right hand was gripping an empty bottle of Jameson's.

"Shit," said McGovern. "I thought you were the cops."

"We thought you were Fred Flintstone," said Ratso.

"Fred caught the last dinosaur out of here, apparently," said McGovern, "before we were able to launch our lightninglike attack. As you can see, he turned out the lights before he left."

I reached for the same light switch I'd hit the night before, flicked it on, and saw nothing but more of the same dim landscape. This was not surprising because the floor was covered with broken glass that had once constituted the lamps and light fixtures. The light from the hallway and the light from the street, however, clearly revealed the massive extent of the damage.

"Mother of God," I said. "The place looks like a war zone."

"I can't believe," said McGovern, "that the bastard had the balls to break into this place two nights in a row."

"Maybe his social life is slow," said Ratso, as we followed McGovern into the scene of destruction that had once been a dance studio.

"Where's Mick?" I said.

"He's securing the perimeter," said McGovern. "Look, Kink, do you think Winnie has any idea who this character is?"

"That's what we have to find out, Watson," I said. "Otherwise, the third time will be the charm."

"Wait a minute, Kinkstah," said Ratso, "I thought *I* was Watson."

"You *are* Watson."

"I thought *I* was Watson," laughed McGovern.

"You *are* Watson."

"We can't *both* be Watson," said Ratso, tucking the knife awkwardly inside his belt like a Jewish pirate.

"Of course you can, my dear Ratso," I said. "You're Watson. McGovern's Watson. Winnie's Watson. President Clinton is Watson. The Chinese dwarf who paints pastels on Mott Street is Watson. The world is Watson. Only Sherlock Holmes stands achingly alone on the weather-beaten, worm-eaten cross of rational thought. Sherlock Holmes, you see, is the thinking man's Jesus Christ."

"Thank you, Seymour Glass," said Ratso.

"Mick!" shouted McGovern. "Come on out! The Japs have surrendered! The war is over!"

Suddenly, an incandescent, atomic-bomb-like flash dazed our senses in the dimness. From the direction of the bedroom, a dark figure moved swiftly toward us. In one hand it still held a camera, in the other, a knife. By the time I realized it wasn't Mick Brennan, it was already too late.

The next thing I knew, a bottle of Jameson's was flying right at me, followed immediately by a large Irish poet who was still attached to the bottle. This left only Ratso standing between the guy and the door, which was, apparently, the mode of egress he had in mind, if he had a mind. I got only a bare glimpse of the guy because McGovern's body was coming toward me at about a hundred miles an hour, crushing me to the floor and burying me like a football quarterback. Though I was at the bottom of the pile, I could still hear but what I heard was even more unsettling.

I once saw an interview with Terry Bradshaw, former Pittsburgh Steeler great, about his impressions of the play sometimes known as the "immaculate reception." For non–football fans, he'd thrown a long, last-second, game-winning pass and had been buried immediately in a pile of bodies. Bradshaw did not know that the ball had bounced off one player's helmet, glanced off another player's chest, then sailed incredibly right into the arms of Pittsburgh's Franco Harris, who was simply trailing the play. Harris ran the ball another thirty yards or so, and to the astonishment of everyone, won the game for the Steelers.

Bradshaw, on his back and covered with about twelve or so McGoverns, couldn't see a thing but could hear the huge roar of the home crowd, which had told him the pass must've been completed. Bradshaw says when he heard the crowd, only one thought was going through his head. The thought was: "Bradshaw, you old son-of-a-gun. You threaded the needle again."

This, of course, is football lingo for a perfect pass. It will not be meaningful, much less humorous, if your life isn't empty enough for you to be a fan of pro football. I've never myself been a true football fan; I just like watching the players tump over on the field.

The point of this dreary Dole-Kemp football analogy is not what I did not see, but what I heard. And when you can't see, what you hear becomes truly indelible. I heard the intruder shouting curses as he fled. I heard his footsteps running across the loft and out the door. And I heard Ratso scream out in a strange, strangled voice: "Oh, God! I've been stabbed!"

28

"WHAT does *where* I got stabbed have to do with it?" Ratso asked sometime later, as he was recuperating on my couch downstairs. "I want to know if my Watson Health Insurance covers my injury."

"It's a big injury to cover," said McGovern, who was nursing Ratso. "I'll have to go over your policy with Sherlock here."

"What about me, mate?" shouted Brennan from the kitchen, where he was busy pouring my new liquor supply down his neck. "I should qualify for Watson Health Insurance, too. I got knocked on the head by that bloke in the bedroom. I was totally out of it for half an hour."

"You've been totally out of it for half your life," said McGovern.

"Bollocks!" said Brennan. "It wouldn't have happened if you'd had the bloody balls to check the bloody bedroom yourself instead of telling me to pop in there."

"But he wasn't *stabbed*, Kinkstah!" said Ratso, rising up from the couch somewhat melodramatically. "I've been *stabbed!* Doesn't that count for anything?"

"Of course it counts, my dear Ratso," I said calmly. "All I'm saying is that the Watson Health Insurance Plan to date has handled very few cases of individuals who've been stabbed in the buttocks by falling on their own knives. We'll have to take this matter under review at another time. Now describe the attacker again, please."

"I've told you this shit already, Kinkstah. I'd say the guy was probably in his thirties. He wore a Lone Ranger mask. Tall, medium build, dark hair. He had what you Texans would call a New York accent, but it's slightly different from the area I grew up in. Maybe a nearby neighborhood."

"Too bad we don't have Professor Higgins here," I said, "to pinpoint the bastard."

"He was coming right at me with the knife," said Ratso. "What I can't understand is why he didn't kill me."

"Quite simple, my dear Ratso," I said. "It isn't you he wants to kill."

It was around Cinderella time, with McGovern and Brennan having departed, and Ratso crashing for the night on his stomach on the couch, when Stephanie called. She and Winnie had returned moments ago, she said, and she'd been with her when they'd confronted the shambles of her dance studio. I told her I was coming up, ready or not; she told me "not." I told her I was coming up anyway. As I left the loft, Ratso was sleeping peacefully and the cat was staring at him balefully. I left the cat in charge.

"I've got to check the chicks," Stephanie told me at the door to Winnie's place.

"Pyramus and Thisbe?"

"They're the only chicks I have, dickhead. Baby Savannah's not arriving for a few more days."

"I just thought you might have some two-legged chicks over there."

"Funny. You'd better talk to Winnie. She's waiting for you in the kitchen."

"Is she all right?"

"No, dickhead. Somebody's just trashed her whole fucking apartment and if she'd been home earlier, he probably would've killed her."

"I don't think so."

"Well, I'm sure she'll be glad to hear that, deerstalker-dick."

"How's she taking it?"

"Better than any man I've ever met," said Stephanie, as she marched across the hall to her apartment.

Winnie was sitting in the kitchen, sipping her usual Red Zinger tea and smoking a Players cigarette. Her eyes were clear and her voice was strong.

"Sit down," she said. "Sorry the place is a mess."

"He came in the front door, Winnie," I said, pulling up a chair. "He picked the lock."

"I don't even know why we have locks in New York."

"To put on bagels," I said.

Winnie laughed a short laugh, careless and sad. "That's about right," she said. "What does this guy want with my life?"

"That's what I'm here to find out. You're pretty sure from last night that you don't know this guy?"

"I've never seen him before in my life."

"Then why does he wear a mask?"

"Everybody wears a mask."

"Fine."

"I don't know."

"What do you think he was looking for in your bedroom? He tore through all the dresser drawers and closets almost like he was searching for something."

"I have no earthly idea. But whatever it is he's looking for, I hope he finds it before he drives away my classes and drives me crazy. Believe me, Kinky, if I knew who he was or why he's doing this to me, I'd tell you."

"I'll say this for him. He's a nervy son-of-a-bitch. Coming back to the same place two nights in a row is really throwing caution to the winds. If he comes back again, knowing our guard is up, it's got to be for blood."

"So what's a girl to do?"

"For one thing, you can cooperate with me fully and let me help you catch him. We almost caught him tonight. He ran out of here wearing a Lone Ranger mask."

"Hiyo, silver lining."

"This may get a little personal here."

"I'll fasten my seat belt."

"How long have you been a lesbian?"

"I was born a lesbian. It just took me a little while to know it."

"But you have had some affairs with men in the past?"

"Not Fred Flintstone."

"How could you tell? He *was* wearing a mask."

"Woman's intuition."

"That's a sexist remark."

"I *am* a sexist. Got a problem with it?"

"No. Everybody's a sexist and everybody wears a mask. But everybody doesn't have some mysterious maniac stalking them. Is it conceivable there's a long-lost lover out there somewhere you've forgotten about?"

"That's another case of everybody. Everybody I've ever loved is a long-lost lover. If they're not now, some day they will be. And no, I've never forgotten any of them."

"You're one smart broad."

"Now that's a sexist remark. Any other questions before you go?"

"You and I had a little fling once."

"That's not a question, and you're making it sound like more than it was. But I haven't forgotten. Repressed is more like it."

"At least I'm not the sole reason you're a lesbian today."

"Don't flatter yourself and don't blame yourself. You weren't my first cowboy and this ain't my first rodeo. If the Lord hadn't wanted me to be what I am, She wouldn't have made me this way. The last man I probably truly ever loved was my dad. He raised me to be a tomboy and I guess I kind of took it from there."

"Amelia Earhart's father raised her to be a tomboy, too, you know."

"If she were around today I'd bet she'd be a lesbian."

"I'm not so sure. She spent a lot of time in the cockpit."

"Christ, men are tiresome."

"Okay, we're almost through for tonight. Just tell me a little more about you and your dad."

"There's not much to say. He let me dress like I wanted. He let me be who I was. He took me fishing on Sundays instead of church. He died when I was twelve."

"And what happened to the tomboy?"

"She grew up. Or maybe she didn't. You know that scene in *Huckleberry Finn* where Huck is on the run and he has to disguise himself?"

"Yeah. He dresses up like a girl."

"That's me."

29

Two days later, on a cold, gray Thursday morning, Ratso's buttocks had healed, apparently, to the point where he felt he could cease being my housepest and finally go home. Though the cat, of course, was in a shamelessly celebratory mood, Ratso had, rather surprisingly, been an almost exemplary housepest. Sustaining himself with a large to-go order I'd picked up at Big Wong's, Ratso positioned himself on the couch to allow him to monitor the bugging device when I was gone or asleep, one of which I was for much of the duration of his stay.

Winnie still did not want the cops. She had, in fact, entrusted the capturing of Fred Flintstone to me, a burden that I quite consciously carried around my neck like a large albatross. I had taken a few precautions, however. I even had a barely embryonic little plan beginning to fertilize in some half-forgotten Freudian field of my fevered brain. The only way to catch Flintstone, or the Lone Ranger, or whoever the hell he was, I figured, was to deliberately trap him. But I couldn't trap him without identifying him. And I couldn't identify him without knowing who or what it was he was actually after.

The only way to trap him, I felt, was to lure him back at such a time as our firepower was at least a match for his own. That meant waiting until Rambam had chased some octogenarian Nazis around some maple trees and returned to New York, which, by my calculations, could happen by the weekend. My goal was to discover the mysterious intruder's identity by that time. My first step in that direction was to call McGovern.

"How's my favorite Watson doing today?" I asked, once I'd gotten him on the line.

"Better than most of your other favorite Watsons," he said. "My butt and my head are in better shape anyway. But I'm worried about Winnie. What are you doing to protect her?"

"I'm keeping the receiver on twenty-four hours a day. I've been in touch regularly by phone with her. And we've established an emergency signal call she can send me as well as a Tony Orlando knock-three-times-on-the-ceiling approach if she needs me."

"Sort of a Lesbian-In-Trouble Hotline."

"Correct. Now look, McGovern, I need some information and you're in the best position to obtain it. Can you get me the names, ages, and a little biographical data on each of Winnie's girls?"

"Jesus, there must be thirty broads in there. I thought I was supposed to interview Winnie."

"The assignment has changed."

"I can tell when you're onto something. This is important, right?"

"It may be of singular importance, Watson. Indeed, it may be vital to solving this investigation."

"It's also possible," I said to the cat, once I'd cradled the blower, "that it may be a crock of shit."

McGovern had promised to get me the information as soon as possible. In the meantime, all I could do was hope that I was on the right track. If I was on the wrong track, Winnie could be in even graver danger than she already was. Winnie's stalker had not provided many clues to his identity, but he had left a few little threads and I hoped to hell they would lead me out of the labyrinth.

There was nothing I could do about the lesbian matter at the moment, so for fun and diversion, I figured I'd get back to work on my fascinating little intellectual puzzle of how Baby Hyena could've croaked before I'd rescued her in the bank. Vinnie and Gepetto had become increasingly erratic in showing up for work lately, which was just as well. It wouldn't be best foot forward to even be muttering the name Tortellini into the blower while they were there.

At first it seemed that before I'd find the oldest Catholic hospital in Brooklyn I might become the oldest Jew in Manhattan, but it didn't take as long as I'd expected. Before Gary Cooper time, I had the phone numbers of the oldest hospital and two runners-up. I felt pretty sure that records from thirty years ago were still in existence; the challenge was to get those daunting institutions to divulge the information to a layman like myself who wasn't a doctor and wasn't a priest and didn't even want to be one when he grew up.

"Our Lady of the Kneecap," said the voice on the blower. "Sister Fra Diavolo speaking."

"This is Dr. Jack Finkelstein from Dallas," I said, in as busy and officious tones as possible. "I need a bone-marrow type-match for a patient and Southwest Airlines has managed to lose my luggage, which, of course, contained the patient file—"

"I'll transfer you to Records, Doctor."

"Fine." I waited a moment or two and finally the line went dead.

"Looks like Kent Perkins's plan is off to a fairly weak start," I said to the cat, as I took a fresh cigar out of Sherlock's head. I dialed the hospital again.

"Our Lady of the Kneecap," said the voice. "Sister Mary Spumoni speaking."

"What happened to Sister Fra Diavolo?" I said.

"She's on a lunch break. Can I help you?"

"I hope so," I said. "This is Dr. Jack Finkelstein from Dallas and I'm running out of time for a bone-marrow match. Can you transfer me to Records, please?"

"Right away, Doctor."

This time the call transferred faster than I could perform the *bris* on my Cuban cigar. It was a good thing, too, because I'd only been Dr. Jack Finkelstein for about five minutes and I was already starting to dislike myself.

"Records," said an older voice. "Sister Constance Rigatoni."

"Sister, this is Dr. Jack Finkelstein from B'nai Ahasueras in Dallas. I'm running out of time on a bone-marrow match for a patient. I must have the certificate of live birth of my patient's sibling to verify a type-match."

"The sibling was born at this hospital?"

"That's right, sister."

"When was the baby born?"

"A little over thirty years ago."

"Did you say thirty, Dr. Finkelman?"

"That's 'stein,' 'stein,' Finkel*stein*. Yes, thirty years ago, sister."

"Our records go back only twenty-five years. I'll have to transfer you to Archives, Dr. Fink—"

I was placed on hold.

"Stein, stein, Finkel*stein*," I chanted to the cat. "Why can't they get it right?"

I was trying to decide whether Jews were more tedious than Catholics or Catholics were more tedious than Jews, when Archives came on the line. This time the sister's voice sounded so old I was afraid she was dead.

"Archives," she said. "Sister Ulalia Eucharist. Are you Dr. Finkelstein?"

"No, I'm Dr. Felch with Catholic Services. I'm working with Dr. Finkelstein, who was just called into surgery."

"How can I help you, Dr. Felch?"

"We need birth information on a baby born probably thirty-one or thirty-two years ago; we're trying to make a bone-marrow match with her sibling, our patient. Our patient is sixteen or seventeen years older than his baby sister and he'd left home long before she was born. He made a different lifestyle choice and has not stayed in touch with his family, so he doesn't even know his sister's given name or her current whereabouts. But the family's name is Tortellini. This really is a matter of grave urgency. It's life or death. Would you mind checking your files for a Tortellini born sometime over thirty years ago? I can't tell you what a blessing it would be if you could find this record for us."

There was silence on the line. Sister Ulalia, very possibly, had fallen asleep. The cat certainly had nodded off. It'd been a long and somewhat laborious entreaty, and frankly I was feeling rather a strong sense of ennui myself. Sister Ulalia had still not said a word.

"Sister?" I said.

I heard a cough somewhere in the background so I assumed she was still alive.

"Sister?"

I heard the sound of creaky old file cabinets opening and closing, so I assumed that at least she was ambulatory. I puffed on the cigar and waited patiently. Alive and ambulatory was good enough for me. After about the length of the Spanish Inquisition, she came back on the line.

"Are you Dr. Felch or Dr. Finkelstein?" she asked.

"Dr. Felch."

"I think I have what you're looking for, Dr. Felch, but we're not allowed to give this information over the phone."

"I understand, sister. If it's all right, I'd like to come by this afternoon and verify the file for a type-match."

"That will be fine, Dr. Felch. Did you tell me you were with

Catholic Services?"

"That's correct, sister."

"And you are of the faith yourself?"

"Yes I am, sister."

"Would you mind asking Dr. Finkelstein a question for me?"

"I'd be glad to just as soon as he gets out of surgery. What's the question?"

"Why did his people kill our Lord?"

30

MOST cab drivers in Manhattan don't want to drive a fare to Brooklyn. This usually works out pretty well because most people in Manhattan don't want to go to Brooklyn in the first place. If you're in Manhattan, however, and you find yourself wishing to perform the unnatural act of taking a cab to Brooklyn, you do have a rather gnarly problem. If you just hail a hack and say "Brooklyn," the cabbie invariably will say "I'm off duty," or at least that's what he'll say if he speaks that much English. So you've got to get in the cab first and close the door and sit there if you're going to have any chance at all. The driver, quite understandably, is concerned that you will get off in Brooklyn and he'll be left without a fare back to Manhattan. If you tell him you want him to wait for you and then take you back, you're really stretching the bounds of credibility. In the end, you've got to promise him your firstborn son, give him a lot of money, and then listen to him bitch all the way to Brooklyn. It's a little bit, so I'm told, like being married.

Vinnie and Gepetto had rolled in for work just about the same time I was grabbing my hat and coat and reaching into Sherlock's head to get a few cigars for the road. I didn't tell them where I was going, of course, mainly because I didn't want to come back and find a fireplace in my bed. There was a strange sort of trust developing between the two Italian workers and myself, however. Indeed, I'd even given Vinnie a key to the loft. I made this gesture primarily on the basis of his close personal relationship with the cat. That, and the fact that it would save wear and tear on the puppet head, with whom Vinnie also seemed to have a close personal relationship.

Anyone who had a close personal relationship with a cat and a puppet head was very possibly clinically ill, I reflected, but not necessarily all bad, present company excluded, of course. My present company was a cab driver from Pakistan. Even he didn't want to go to Brooklyn, and he manifested this disinclination by driving as recklessly as everyone else and by carrying on a long, loud irritating conversation on his radio with a guy in Pakistani. By the time we got to the Williamsburg Bridge, he was still yapping away in Pakistani to the guy, and it was beginning to get up my sleeve rather severely.

"C'mon, you're in America," I said. "Speak Spanish."

Every hospital in the world has two things in common with every other hospital in the world. One: They all smell like a hospital, and Two: If you stay there long enough, you'll die. If you stay in a lot of places long enough, you'll die. You could die of ennui at a bar mitzvah reception or a condominium board meeting. But very few places indeed have that ubiquitous, pervasive, peculiarly antiseptic odor redolent of stale farts, stale perfume, dying flowers, and dying people.

Fortunately, I didn't plan to stay in this hospital long enough to sniff the cork. All I needed was a couple of minutes with the Tortellini file and I'd be out of here faster than a doctor leaves to play golf. I left the cowboy hat as collateral with the Pakistani driver, and I made an emergency bypass of the front desk, popping instead into the doctors' lounge. On a nearby table was a large pile of cleanly pressed lime-green scrub suits and funny little lime-green doctor's hats or surgical skypieces or whatever you were supposed to wear when you pinch the nurse on the ass and shout, "Scalpel."

Impersonating a doctor is not as serious as impersonating a cop or impersonating a woman, just as long as you don't try to prescribe drugs, or attempt to transplant a heart into the Tin Man, or try to remove the patient's wallet. I stepped quickly out of the doctors' lounge and soon found myself moving about the hospital with a nice little aura of self-importance. A stethoscope carelessly hung around my neck like a yuppie's sweater would've been nice, but you can't have everything.

It didn't take long for Dr. Felch to find Sister Ulalia Eucharist in the building's dusty old basement Archives department. She looked like a Grim Reaper who'd lost his scythe. I had to admire, however, how she still kept going, in her decrepit state, after all these years. Some of the best human rocket fuel known to man, unquestionably, is institutionalized ignorance. I didn't know why Jack Finkelstein's people killed her Lord. Maybe they did it for the life insurance. The first recorded case of Jewish lightning. Maybe it was simply some kind of perverse social experiment to see if, thousands of years later, Sister Ulalia would spend her life hating Jews while simultaneously praying to one.

The good sister had no problem in directing Dr. Felch to the Tortellini file. It was yellowed and dusty and looked like the Magna Carta on a bad hair day. But it contained the information Dr. Felch had come there to find. The little girl had been born on July 23, 1964. Fairly cosmic, thought Dr. Felch. July 23 was also Don Imus's birthday. It was also Kacey Cohen's birthday. Maybe it wasn't Jewish lightning, he reflected, as he wondered at the star-crossed nature of the timing of Baby Hyena's birth. Of course, her name was not really Baby Hyena. It was Genovese Maria Tortellini. And the Priest who'd presided at the birth, and no doubt returned three days later to sprinkle holy water on the infant, was Father Patrick O'Sullivan.

31

THAT'S what happens sometimes when you go chasing windmills," I said.

"That's what also happens sometimes," said Rambam, "when you go chasing Nazis."

It was a shivery Saturday afternoon and, with Rambam just back from Canada, we were discussing how to capture Fred Flintstone alive and how to verify that Genovese Maria Tortellini was dead.

"I still prefer Baby Hyena," Rambam was saying.

"Well, that's not her name. Her name is—or was—Genovese Maria Tortellini."

"That's a mouthful," said Rambam. "But I wouldn't get too attached to the notion of her being alive. She's probably worm bait in some family cemetery somewhere. If Joe the Hyena says his daughter is dead, who are we to argue with him?"

"I never said she was alive. Just indulge me with this little hobby of mine. It's the only hobby I have—"

"What about smoking cigars?"

"That's not a hobby. That's a religion. All I want to find out is if Baby Hyena—"

"Genovese Maria Tortellini."

"Okay. All I want to find out is if Genovese Maria Tortellini died three years before I rescued her from the mugger, like Vinnie says, why did Joe the Hyena send me his eternal gratitude and this espresso machine from which we are currently sucking nectar?"

"You're sucking. I'm sipping. Also he didn't send you his eternal gratitude. Nothing is eternal with the mob. It's easy come, easy go, and, believe me, it's mostly easy go. But your little hobby has piqued my curiosity."

"While you were gone, I talked to Kent Perkins in L.A. It was his idea to find the priest and to get him to tell us about his flock."

"With all respect to Kent, finding Patrick O'Sullivan is going to be easy—getting him to talk is another story. Remember, no matter how they gloss it over with religion, his flock is really a pack of hyenas. Is Kent a Catholic?"

"Southern Baptist."

"Close enough. They're all *goyim*. I wouldn't have done it this way, but since it's your only hobby, I'll go along with it. You see, this priest is really part of the family. If he suspects anything, you can count on a visit from Joe the Hyena, and it won't be to see how the work on the ceiling is going."

"As you can see, by the way, the work on the ceiling is almost done. Next, Vinnie and Gepetto are going to put in a fireplace and Joe is paying for it."

"Oh, that's just fucking great. This makes it imperative that Father O'Sullivan doesn't get wise to us. If he does, and Joe the Hyena finds out we're sneaking around behind his back to uncover family secrets, well, fuck. He'll think, if this is how these Jewboys show their gratitude—"

"For what? An espresso machine and a fireplace that isn't built yet? I saved his daughter, remember?"

"I remember. Just ask yourself how important is your little hobby?"

"My hobby is my life."

"It might come to that. Ask yourself another question. Which would the two of us enjoy more: sitting here on a cold winter's night sipping espresso by the fireplace—"

"Or?"

"Or sharing a pair of matching rent-a-car trunks at JFK?"

"Surely you're overdramatizing. I can't believe a big ol' Nazi hunter like yourself is nervous about paying a little undercover visit to a Catholic priest."

"I didn't say I wouldn't do it," said Rambam. "All I said was that your little hobby could turn out to be extremely fucking dangerous."

As the afternoon grew colder and darker, I nursed a few more rounds of espresso out of the gleaming dingus that took up most of my kitchen and now seemed to be taking over much of my life. I related to Rambam the "Return of the Lone Ranger" incident of earlier in the week, which he found quite humorous, especially the part about Ratso stabbing himself in the buttocks with the kitchen knife.

"It's pretty much a waiting game now," I said. "I've given Mc-Govern a crucial assignment and I'm keeping a close watch on Winnie and she's cooperating. I think things are going to come to a head pretty soon, though, and I'll definitely need your help if we're going to nab this guy."

"Jesus," said Rambam. "Am I getting paid for this?"

"In the coin of the spirit, my friend."

"To help a lonely lesbian in Lower Manhattan?"

"No," I said. "To help a lonely Jewboy in Lower Baboon's Asshole."

"Speaking of Lower Baboon's Asshole, we did manage to locate some old men in Canada who still tied their shoes with little Nazis. Many of them have shot hundreds of Jewish and Gypsy children to death in ditches and were enjoying their retirement until Joey Schacter and I came along. I think I told you, they were so confident nobody'd ever fuck with them they didn't even bother to change their names. We found them in the phone book."

"And you talked to them?"

"Talked to them? I wore a wire and interviewed them, pretending to be a professor from a nonexistent university in Belize. They told me all about it, showed me pictures of themselves in their SS uniforms, and let me take photos of them with their old guns. Now the shit storm has started and the heat's on them and it won't be as easy next time. Of course, there's about one chance in a thousand that any legal action will be successful against them, but at least they'll spend a little more time now looking nervously over their shoulders."

"Not much of a punishment."

"It certainly isn't. But we definitely put them in the spotlight and they hate that more than anything. You want to come with me next time?"

"Next time? Wouldn't all this publicity have alerted them by now?"

"Sure. That's the challenge of Nazi hunting in Canada. Now, Australia is virgin territory and there's lots of Nazis down there, too."

"What about South America? You always hear about nests of Nazis down there."

"South America's more expensive and more dangerous. We'd have to hire backup. Four guys with automatic weapons. That sort of thing. I think we'd have more fun in Australia. Also, we'd have a better chance of coming back alive."

"And I bet Piers Akerman would go with us. I'll make you a deal. If you'll help me catch this Fred Flintstone fuck who's been terrorizing our lesbian sisters—"

"*Your* lesbian sisters—"

"—and go to confession with me at Father O'Sullivan's Church of the Latter Day Businessman, I'll go to Australia with you to hunt Nazis. Is it a deal?"

"It's about the sickest deal anybody ever heard of, but you're on," said Rambam. "I've already got an idea for how we can approach Father O'Sullivan."

"Care to share it with the rest of the class?"

"Sorry, Sherlock. As you, of all people, should know, I never reveal my methods."

As the dark shadows were stretching across the narrow vista of Vandam Street, Rambam got up, stretched himself, and began walking around the place like a caged animal, which, no doubt, part of him was. This was always a rather clear signal that he was preparing to leave the premises. Suddenly, I remembered something I wanted to tell him.

"By the way, the receiver here is working just fine. The reason it's been silent is that Winnie's resting from a rather traumatic week. But this Fred Flintstone guy, when he returned as the Lone Ranger—"

"Listen to how crazy that sounds."

"Almost as crazy as Nazi hunting in Australia. But get this. He said something pretty interesting before we all went up to try to catch him."

"If he said, 'Betcha can't catch me,' he was right."

"This is serious, Rambam. Over this very receiver, we heard him say: 'Your father can't save you. Nobody can save you. If I can't have you, nobody can.' "

"Typical O. J. Simpson murderous bullshit," said Rambam. "What's so unusual about that?"

"I'll tell you what's so unusual," I said. "Winnie's father died when she was twelve years old."

32

I F you spend a little time with lesbians and nuns, you begin to see the effect love or the absence of it can have on a human life. The lesbians or the nuns will change before your very eyes from creatures of curiosity, freaks of human nature, to compact, complete, walled-in, breathing entities, possessed of a peace of mind you almost envy. And, upon closer scrutiny, you will find that the apparent differences between the two tend to intermingle and disappear in time like human sweat mixing quite naturally with holy water.

For what is a nun, if not a spiritual lesbian? And what is a lesbian, if not a sexual nun? And what is a man, if he can't respect, admire, and wonder how they can possibly get along without him? For his very absence is one of the things that makes them who they are. The time a woman spends picking up the pieces of a man's life after him might be better used loving Jesus or loving herself, which is tantamount to the same thing as Gertrude Stein and Mother Teresa grow closer every day until they are as indistinguishable as Italian and Jewish grandmothers and become essentially sisters of one big soul.

"Every sinner has a future," I said to the cat. "Every saint has a past."

The cat did not seem vastly interested in my theological musings. She seemed to recognize, possibly better than I did myself, the hypocrisy that resided within me. Obviously, however lofty were my thoughts or my dreams, I would never be a candidate for the College of Cardinals. The cat, for a reason that was quite understandable, had long dreamed of herself being in the College of Cardinals. The reason was she wanted to eat one.

The weekend crawled to a close like a non-goal-oriented tortoise, and I must confess to feeling pretty much the same way about things myself. To start a fire in the fireplace, first you had to have a fireplace. I still had no clue to the intruder's identity, nor did I know when he might decide to strike again. Even if Winnie succeeded in alerting me that an attack was under way, I was not really equipped to collar the perpetrator. To set an effective trap, you had to make contact with the rat or at least find out what bait he liked, neither of which seemed likely at the moment.

As far as defensive measures for the lesbian enclave were concerned, with her classes and the various Village Irregulars still trooping up there on a regular basis, the only real time of danger, I felt, was late at night. The two previous attacks had occurred in the wee hours, and if another one were to happen, I strongly suspected the timing would be the same. All this meant was that I now had to stay up practically till dawn like a night watchman monitoring some crazy kind of dick-meter in order to protect a bunch of lesbians. It was a dirty job and I got to do it.

There also existed the possibility, of course, that our little SWAT team had spooked the guy so thoroughly that he'd never be back. But guys like that are like herpes or bad memories—if you wait long enough, they always come back, and in this case, I didn't think we'd have to wait very long. That was why I'd made the rather pathetic gesture of leaving Winnie my baseball bat. Not that she wasn't a brave, formidable presence all alone, but even a lesbian with a baseball bat isn't bulletproof.

By Monday night I was preparing to hang myself by the heels from the espresso machine when several much-awaited developments occurred. The first, in order of chronology, was McGovern's knock on the door.

"Come in, Watson," I said.

"I can't," said McGovern. "The door is locked."

"Right you are, Watson," I said. "I was just testing your powers of observation."

"How'd you know it was me?" asked McGovern, once I'd ushered him in and sat him down in my almost perpetually empty client's chair. "It could've been anybody."

"Hardly, Watson, hardly. I've made quite a study of the distinctive styles different persons have employed when knocking upon the door to this particular loft. A person smaller than you, which, unfortunately, includes just about everybody, might knock at a higher physical point on the door just to compensate for his size. A tall person might knock from the hip, and thusly seem shorter. So you see, it is a study of the personality of the knocker himself or herself. Ratso raps rapaciously to get in, much like a rat. Brennan raps belligerently yet playfully. He might beat a little coda on the door. Rambam is forceful, but professional in his approach. Stephanie is also forceful, yet feminine, sometimes slightly employing the use of her long nails almost like timpani. You yourself knock in a polite, at times somewhat hesitant, fashion, indicating the self-effacing nature of a big, strong man with a measure of sensitivity that more than matches his size. As you can imagine, it's quite a fascinating little science."

McGovern appeared to be asleep in the chair. I went over to the espresso machine, sucked out two double shots of espresso, brought them back to the desk, and shook him awake.

"Oh, sorry," he said. "I've had a long day interviewing lesbians."

"Well, at least it's work. Did you have a hard time getting them to open up, so to speak?"

"Hell no," said McGovern, warming to the subject. "That was the amazing thing. They'll tell the *Times* of London things they'd never breathe a word of to their local paper. I've got their biographical data all here for you, including a photo of each that Brennan rushed through in his own darkroom."

"You guys are really on the ball," I said. "This could be a big help in finding the guy who, sometimes quite literally, has been making such a mess of Winnie's life. These are a priceless investigative tool, Watson."

"Do you really think so?"

"But of course, my dear Watson, but of course."

I looked through a few of the thirty or so biographical sketches rather cursorily, and then began checking through some of the photographs Brennan had taken. I wasn't sure if this was a priceless investigative tool or a total tissue of horseshit, but I had to admit that I was taken by a number of the photographs.

"You know," said McGovern, "when I started this, I expected to find tough, jaded, big-city types. But many of these girls come from little towns all over America. Take away a few fashionably butch hairstyles, and you can see for yourself how innocent, youthful, fresh, and feminine they truly are."

"The girls next door," I said.

"That's what I was thinking," said McGovern.

At this rather poignant interlude, a highly agitato, rapacious rapping sound reverberated upon the door of the loft.

"Come in, Watson," I said.

"Open up, Kinkstah!" shouted the voice in the hallway. "The fucking door is locked."

"Just testing your powers of patience and perception, my dear Watson," I said, as I guided Ratso into the loft.

He nodded at McGovern, walked over to the refrigerator, found it to be empty, came back to the desk, and started flipping through the photographs.

"What have we got here?" said Ratso excitedly. "Hot babes!"

"Watson," I said, "you always cease to amaze me."

"They may call themselves lesbians," said Ratso, rubbing his hands together like an insect, "but turn 'em upside down and they're all the same."

It was later that night, long after Ratso and McGovern had taken their leave, that the phones began ringing with a strange and singular urgency. I picked up the blower on the left.

"Start talkin'," I said.

"Dere a guy named Kinky dere?" said an overly gruff, obviously disguised voice.

"Who wants to know?" I said, sharing a quick, nervous glance with the cat.

"Dis is Joe Bananas," said the voice.

"Yes, Rambam, I have no bananas," I said.

It pretty much had to be Rambam. The only dead mobster that I ever heard of calling anybody on the blower was a guy named Leaning Jesus. As fate would have it, he'd called Mc-Govern.

"Meet me tomorrow," said Rambam, "at Positano's on Mulberry Street in Little Italy. Say one o'clock. We'll have lunch there and then proceed just down the street to the Church of the Most Precious Blood where Father Patrick O'Sullivan will receive us."

"That's great," I said. "Fast work."

"We aim to keep the customer satisfied."

"Just one question," I said. "Are we going to be Jewish or are we going to be Catholic?"

"That," said Rambam, "we leave in the hands of God."

33

KINKSTAH!" said Ratso the following morning, as I almost broke my neck getting to the blower. "I've got some more information on Le Petomane!"

"Timely, Watson, very timely," I said with a marked lack of enthusiasm. The espresso machine was cold. I was cold. The world was cold.

"I found a rare old edition down at the Strand Bookstore. It's an account by Le Petomane's eldest son, Louis Pujol, describing his father's opening night at the Moulin Rouge in 1892. He went on to play a twenty-two-year engagement there, which is almost as long as your engagement at the Lone Star."

"But it seems like yesterday." I still wasn't sure if I agreed with the Beatles, who said "I believe in yesterday," or with the Stones, who said "Yesterday don't matter when it's gone." Probably, they were both right.

"Listen to this," said Ratso. "It's Louis Pujol recalling his father Joseph's words: 'My children, I never had stage fright before going on—not even on my opening night at the Moulin Rouge.

" 'Ladies and gentlemen,' Le Petomane told the crowd, 'I have the honour to present a session of Petomanie. The word Petomanie means someone who can break wind at will but don't let your nose worry you. My parents ruined themselves scenting my rectum.' Now the son describes witnessing that first performance. 'During the initial silence, my father coolly began a series of small farts, naming each one.'

" 'This one is a little girl, this the mother-in-law, this the bride on her wedding night (very little) and the morning after (very loud), this the mason (dry—no cement), this the dressmaker tearing two yards of calico (this one lasted at least ten seconds and imitated to perfection the sound of material being torn), then a cannon (Gunners stand by your guns! Ready—fire!), the noise of thunder, etc., etc.'

" 'Then my father would disappear behind the scenes for a moment to insert the end of a rubber tube such as are used for enemas. It was about a yard long and he would take the other end in his fingers and in it place a cigarette which he lit. He would then smoke the cigarette as if it were in his mouth, the contraction of his muscles causing the cigarette to be drawn in and then the smoke blown out. Finally my father removed the cigarette and blew out the smoke he had taken in. He then placed a little flute with six stops in the end of the tube and played one or two little tunes such as "Le Bon Roi Dagobert" and of course "Au Clair de la Lune." To end the act, he removed the flute and then blew out several gas jets in the footlights with some force.' "

"Bravo!" I said.

"That's what the audience said, too. Listen to this: 'The mad laughter soon built up into general applause. The public and especially women fell about laughing. They would cry from laughing. Many fainted and fell down and had to be resuscitated.' "

"Must be an old book to include that material. Women today don't seem to find farting particularly humorous."

"Women today don't seem to find anything particularly humorous. In fact, nobody today seems to find anything particularly humorous."

"Ah, my dear Watson, to paraphrase Oscar Wilde—and what clever thing can be said without paraphrasing Oscar Wilde—'Life is too important to be taken seriously.' "

"Why do you think I'm helping you with your investigation of the lesbian dance class?"

"I think, unfortunately, you are motivated by a more personal and I must say, rather misguided, notion."

"Which is?"

"To get laid, my dear Watson, to get laid."

"Hey, Kinkstah. If it happens, it happens. I recognize what I'm up against."

"To paraphrase Emily Dickinson, 'Hope, my dear Ratso, is the thing with feathers that perches in the soul.' "

"To paraphrase Le Petomane—" said Ratso, as a brief silence occurred on the line. This was followed by a sound that was uncannily similar to that which might've been made by a dressmaker tearing two yards of calico.

34

So first we're Jews," I said to Rambam as we sat at the little table at Positano's, "and then we're Catholics?"

"You'd be surprised how many people actually do it that way," said Rambam grimly.

"Surely you exaggerate."

"I'm not exaggerating. Pretty soon the only Jews left in the world will be the ones wearing funny little black hats."

"Reminds me of the joke John Mankiewicz told me. Two Jews are walking past a Catholic church and there's a sign out front that says: 'Convert To Catholicism! We Pay You $200!' So one of the Jews says he thinks he'll try it and he goes on in. After a while he comes out and they're walking down the street and the other Jew asks him, 'How was it?' and he says, 'Okay.' Then the other Jew asks: 'Did they give you the two hundred dollars?' And he says: 'Is that all you people think about?' "

After Positano's, we took a leisurely stroll down Mulberry Street and ankled a sharp right into the old courtyard of the Church of the Most Precious Blood. I'd agreed to let Rambam do the talking until we actually got on to the subject of Baby

Hyena, the name by which he still seemed fond of referring to her.

"We'd like to see Father O'Sullivan," said Rambam to a kindly-looking nun at the desk.

"Father is very busy today," she said. "If you'd like to make an appointment—"

"Oh, that's all right," said Rambam, preparing to leave. "We're just two guys who were raised as Jews and we were thinking of possibly converting."

"If you'll wait here a moment I'll see what I can do," said the nun, rising from her desk, smiling, and leaving the room.

"Works every time," said Rambam.

A short while later, with Rambam squeezed onto the same small seat beside me, I found myself staring at what little I could see of Father O'Sullivan through the lattice window of a confessional booth. For his part, it is doubtful whether Father O'Sullivan had ever before seen the jigsaw vision of two male faces gazing back at him. Again, Rambam led the way.

"Forgive us, Father, for we have sinned," said Rambam.

"What is it, my son?" asked Father O'Sullivan.

"Father, is it true," said Rambam, "that whatever transpires between yourself and the penitent is totally confidential and can never be told to anyone, anywhere, anytime, whatsoever?"

"Yes, my son," said Father O'Sullivan.

"And anyone who breaks the sacred code of the confessional will go to hell?"

"Purgatory at the very least," said O'Sullivan. "Yes, that is true."

"That's good enough for me," whispered Rambam. "You're up to bat."

"Father," I said, "there is a young girl who may be in grave danger. We don't even know if she's alive or dead. We come to you because we think you can help us, Father."

"How can I help you, my son?"

"You and I know this girl, Father. You brought her into the world. I saved her from a mugger about ten years ago."

"What is this young girl's name, my son?"

"Genovese Maria Tortellini."

"I tried to save her, too, my son. But she drifted away from the Church, from her family, and from the young man to whom she was engaged to be married. It broke the young man's heart. It broke her father's heart. But when it came to how she wanted to live her life, Gena always made her own choices. We may not agree with those choices, but we must respect her right to make them. To my knowledge she is very much alive."

"Thank you, Father O'Sullivan."

"Go in peace, my son."

We went, but not in peace. My mind was whirling with chances and probabilities and the odds of anything at all occurring in that fated, star-crossed, crazy little neighborhood we call the world. Everything told me it *couldn't* be, yet it *had* to be.

As we walked down Mulberry Street, I was oblivious to all the bright and jangly sights and sounds of the city. Are we forever to see destiny and call it coincidence, I wondered? Is the fine Italian hand that paints the masterpiece guided by the hand of God? Can man ever attain the humanity of a Seeing Eye dog? The grace of a lesbian dancer? The ability to know when a trivial hobby leads him into the very smoke of life?

"So who's Gena?" asked Rambam.

"I'm not one hundred percent certain yet," I said, "but I hate nicknames."

"I can see why a guy named Kinky might feel that way."

35

M Y friend Sal Lorello once shared with me a killer-bee Italian dessert known as *zeppole*. According to Sal, it's a dish that is virtually unknown outside of traditional Italian families. "It's not a tourist thing," he'd said of the object that resembled a doughnut without a hole. "It'd probably be not easy to find even in Little Italy." Only in Italy itself, according to Sal, or in old-world Italian families in America, might *zeppole* be a fixture.

"You take a fried hunk of dough," he'd said, "which is not very health-conscious these days, and shake it up in a brown paper bag full of powdered sugar. *Zeppole* simply does not thrive outside of a real Italian neighborhood."

By late that afternoon I'd reached Sal in Chappaqua and managed to convince him that my obtaining some *zeppole* immediately was a matter of life or death. I might've been stretching things a little, but I couldn't take any chances. Sal said if he couldn't find any *zeppole,* he'd come to my loft and fry some up himself that evening. I told him he was a fine American. "Make that a fine Italian-American," he'd said.

So it was that the loft became somewhat of an Italian kitchen that night with paper bags, powdered sugar, and hunks of dough scattered all over the counter, and with the espresso machine humming and gurgling away and looking happier than it had in years.

"You're sure this is a matter of life or death?" asked Sal, as he proceeded to make extremely elaborate preparations for what would appear to be one of your more basic dishes.

"Positive," I said. "You're sure that only an Italian would know about this *zeppole* stuff?"

"Many Italians never heard of it," said Sal. "But a *real* Italian would know for sure."

"That's what I'm counting on," I said, as I studied Brennan's photograph of a lesbian named Gena Lake who listed her hometown as Manhattan, Kansas. That was a nice touch, I thought. Gays seemed to be the only people in the world who romanticized Kansas. They knew it was so boring that God shaped it like a square, placed it right in the middle of the broad buttocks of the country like a giant Oz-hole dumping out Dorothy and the dog and her freaky, fetishist, red stilettoes just in time for Judy Garland to die on a toilet in London like Elvis or Lenny Bruce, no doubt wishing she were back in Kansas. Kansas was the perfect place for people who didn't fit in anywhere to be from, including myself. Kansas was everything you couldn't carry with you and really didn't want to. Kansas wasn't even a good place to get a postcard from. Many maître d's in the most coochi-poochi-boomalini establishments in New York and Los Angeles were originally from Kansas. They followed Dorothy out, and after a vanilla ice age or two they wanted to go back, but they couldn't leave everywhere else until Andy Warhol wrapped their pâté in a roadmap and Truman Capote lifted his Tiffany lamp beside the golden whore with the waving fields of pain.

"Your father can't help you," I said to Gena Lake's photograph.

"Who's that babe?" asked Sal, temporarily straying from his

zeppole duties to gaze admiringly over my shoulder.

"Just a girl I used to know," I said.

If you've never sampled some of Sal Lorello's *zeppole,* you definitely must've missed the *Mayflower.* Sal took several with him on his way out, Ratso ate about nineteen kilograms on his way upstairs to Winnie's, and even Stephanie DuPont tried a few after I'd finally coaxed her down to the loft, telling her it was a matter of life and death. Of course, just looking at Stephanie in her lesbian leotards was a matter of life and death, and you almost didn't care which.

"This better be good," she said, sitting in the client's chair and crossing the legs that were longer and hotter than summers in Shreveport before Jimmy Swaggart said "Let there be air conditioning."

"You mean the *zeppole?*"

"*Zeppole-schmeppole,*" she said. "I mean this life-and-death shit better be good."

"Here are your instructions, Watson," I said, in brisk, businesslike tones.

"Is that some kind of joke?" she asked. "You pathetic, posturing prick."

"This is no time for banter or small talk, Watson."

" 'Small' being the operative word here."

"Watson, I need your help. I'm afraid these are deep waters."

"Good," she said cheerfully. "Maybe I can drown your ass."

I gave Stephanie her instructions and a bag of *zeppole,* which, of course, was the bait. Sort of an Italian tar baby for the girl I hoped was who I thought she was. If I was correct, then you could truly say it was a small world. You could also bet your Borneo blowpipe that Gena Lake would soon be knocking on my door.

I resurrected an old cigar and poured a generous jolt of Jameson's into the old bull's horn. Before I poured the contents of the bull's horn down my neck, I toasted the cat. "Every dog has his day," I said. "And ours I believe is coming." The cat turned her back on me and stared at the opposite wall. "An unfortunate choice of words," I said. Then I killed the shot and quickly poured another into the bull's horn. This time, I walked over to the refrigerator and toasted the friendly little black puppet head. "To fallen comrades," I said. The puppet head's smile did not waver, but something in his wooden stare told me that he liked the toast almost as much as had the cat. "Present company excluded, of course," I said. Then I downed the shot and paced back and forth across the little kitchen for a while, thinking that the trouble with the world today was that too many people took too many things personally.

"What's the matter with you guys?" I said, somewhat rhetorically, since neither of them seemed to be paying attention at all. "Why can't we all get along with Rodney King?" I paced back and forth between the Jameson bottle, the Texas-shaped ashtray on the desk, and the kitchen window. Sometimes I missed the ashtray altogether and the ashes of the cigar fell to the floor. I didn't care. The world is my ashtray, I thought. And if you live in the world you've got to stop taking things to heart. You've got to learn to pick the racehorses with the least soulful names. "One for the Money" beats "Jacob's Dream" every time. I myself had dreams and memories that perhaps it'd be far better and wiser to let go of. I'd once kissed a beautiful girl on the backs of her knees in the parking lot of a Wal-Mart's in Knoxville, Tennessee, for instance. As Paul Harvey often tells us on the radio: "You'll never have a better neighbor than Wal-Mart."

I was just starting to miss that girl again when, as destiny would have it, the phones rang. I walked over to the desk and quickly collared the blower on the left.

"Vasectomy Reversal World Headquarters," I said. "Hold for a moment, please."

"Kinkstah!" said Ratso. "I'm calling to file a report!"

"Spit it," I said.

"I think your friend Stephanie's having an affair with one of the girls in the dance group. I'm home now. Winnie wasn't feeling well and she called the class early. She's been under a lot of pressure lately."

"So have I, Watson. Pray, continue."

"So as I was leaving I saw Stephanie and this hot redhead go across the hall together and into Stephanie's apartment. They looked very chummy, Sherlock, very chummy."

"Watson, is there anything that evades your eaglelike powers of observation?"

"I guess not, Sherlock. I've even unearthed some additional information on Le Petomane. Listen to this. It's a report from the *Journal de Médecine* of Bordeaux, 20 March, 1892 by Dr. Marcel Baudouin. '. . . Le Petomane can obtain effects which are both as brilliant as they are surprising and unforeseen. When the gas comes out with enough force and with a certain degree of tension from the sphincter, noises are produced of intensity, timbre, and of great variety. At times these are genuinely musical sounds. Although as it is almost impossible to obtain given notes these turn out to be common chords or, what is more extraordinary, recognizable tunes.' "

"This blows me away."

"Wait, Kinkstah! There's more! Dr. Baudouin continues: 'Le Petomane imitates all sorts of sounds such as the violin, the bass and the trombone. He can produce a strong enough note ten or twelve times running and he can take in enough air to produce sound lasting ten or fifteen seconds.' "

"A veritable eternity," I said. "That asshole was a genius."

"And listen to Dr. Baudouin's concluding observation in the laboratory: 'Without clothes the subject can extinguish at a distance of 12 inches, a burning candle, by the force of gas violently expelled from the anus.' "

"Mother of God!" I said. "A candle in the wind!"

Long moments after I'd cradled the blower with Ratso, my

mind was still blown by his account of the scientific documentation of Le Petomane's great talents. In a state of mild wonder, I sat at my desk almost unconsciously going through the Freudian foreplay associated with the breaking in of a fresh cigar. It was at about this time that I heard the rather tentative knock on my door.

"Come in, Genovese," I said.

36

THE only sure way to stop a stalker is to croak him. In my narrow experience, I'd managed to kill a lot of time and a few relationships, but never had I killed a man or consciously caused a person to die, and it was getting a little late in life's chess game to change my strategy now. Gena Lake a/k/a Genovese Maria Tortellini, a/k/a Baby Hyena, had been very open and forthcoming in her little chat with me. She had been carrying her dark secret for a long time and seemed to be relieved to have finally unburdened herself. She was frightened, of course, and with very good reason. The mad stalker, as I had suspected for some time, had never been after Winnie. It was Gena he'd been after, and indications were that he definitely intended to continue to stalk her until he found the chance to kill her.

As for who the stalker was, Gena had suspected all along that it might be him but hadn't known for sure until one recent night when she'd spotted him on Vandam Street. He'd spotted her as well, and she'd run back up to Winnie's for safety. He was the man she'd virtually left at the altar when she'd made the "choices" that Father Patrick O'Sullivan had spoken of. The choices had been to become a lesbian, to leave this proud young Italian stallion from another powerful mob family, and to cause her own father, Joe the Hyena, such grief that he told the world, "My daughter is dead."

"Now all we have to do," I said to the cat after Gena had left, "is make sure Joe the Hyena remains wrong in his pronouncement."

The cat, of course, said nothing. She did not approve of alternative lifestyles in general and did not countenance Italian cats going around saying "ciao" instead of "meow."

Over the next few days, however, there was a lot of work for me to do. I talked with Winnie in private and explained the situation to her. I talked with Rambam several times about the precise mechanism to catch and punish a man named Michael Linguini for a crime the cops were often powerless to prevent. "The best you'd get from the cops would probably be a restraining order," Rambam had said, "and a restraining order has never managed to restrain anyone."

It was decided at last that Rambam and I would approach Vinnie and Gepetto. We'd lay out the facts about Gena's existence and her imminent danger. On the strength of that, we'd ask them to attempt to appeal to Joe the Hyena for a reconciliation with his daughter. Somewhat surprisingly, they were warm to the idea and even offered to "take care of" Michael Linguini if we could catch him in the act of trying to harm Gena. In the meantime, I'd arranged with Stephanie to have Gena move into her place temporarily for safety reasons, thereby generating a mild flurry of rather salacious speculation from Ratso.

My plan was to entice the culprit by engaging the help of Gena's family and leaking the word that she'd be alone at Winnie's place on a given night. Just as Gena's instinctive reaction to *zeppole* had convinced Stephanie I was correct in my guess at her identity, Gena herself would now have to be the tar baby that convinced Michael Linguini to make one last stab at it, so to speak. If all went well, Vinnie and Gepetto and the boys would then take him away and dispense upon him their own arcane and surely more effective form of punishment. The only downside of the whole operation, as far as I was concerned, was that Vinnie and Gepetto had finally gotten into high gear, finishing with the ceiling, and almost completing work on the new fireplace. This new distraction could sideline them indefinitely. Possibly it was selfish of me, but I really wanted to see that fireplace finished in my lifetime.

It was a wish I was soon to realize. The wheels of mob justice, and even apparently mob communication, turned exceedingly slow. It was almost a week before word came from the underworld that Michael Linguini had been cleverly conned into believing Gena would be alone at Winnie's loft on the following night. This was done without arousing his suspicion through the services of a mole in Linguini's own family who, it had been learned, had made some alternative lifestyle choices herself. During the week in which all this furtive activity had taken place, Vinnie and Gepetto, to my great joy, had at last put the final touches on the fireplace.

It was the perfect Sherlockian fireplace, set with its back to Vandam Street so you could stir the embers on a wintry day and still catch sight of a loaded Dumpster and a sleeping garbage truck. It was not the giant, roaring fireplace of the ski lodge or hunting lodge set. It was too small for Santa Claus to get down without burning his ass. Too narrow for anyone but the most lithe of chimney sweeps to climb its bricked internal tower, possibly overcome with masturbatory fantasies of Mary Poppins, and there practice various forms of autoerotic asphyxiation. My concern, of course, was that it did not asphyxiate myself and the cat, and that the puppet head, of all people, remain high above the flames on the mantelpiece, smiling happily down upon his own private universe.

The fireplace, it should be noted, had remained untested. In

New York, wood must be purchased at ridiculously inflated prices or scavenged from the street in any form possible, which makes you feel like a character from either Charles Dickens or Victor Hugo depending upon literary bent or political orientation. But the wood could wait, I felt. There was something else present in the loft that should be the first object to be ceremonially burned in the new fireplace.

"The very first thing I intend to burn in our new fireplace," I said to the cat, as night fell upon the city and the loft, "is that damned drunken threatening note that I wrote."

The cat looked on with mild interest. The puppet head beamed his approval from his new perch high on the mantelpiece. I opened the middle drawer of the desk, lifted some piles of papers, and ferreted out the damning document in question.

"The Xeroxed copy the Chinese waiter made was not a very good facsimile. Besides, a copy is merely a copy when all is said and done. For all I know Rambam's probably forgotten about it by now. But the original is the work of the devil and must be destroyed!"

The cat looked on, possibly impressed with my fervor. I took the note over to the fireplace.

"You're the only one who knows that I'm the author of this note," I said to the cat. "Rambam, Ratso, McGovern, Brennan, and Stephanie all believe it was written by a deranged stalker named Michael Linguini. If ever they discovered that I'd written it myself, they'd most assuredly and rightfully feel betrayed. It would mean the end of the Village Irregulars! My friends would all despise me!"

The cat watched with rekindled interest as I placed the note in the empty fireplace. As I lighted a kitchen match against the leg of my jeans, the flame reflected brightly in both of her eyes.

"No one can ever know that I wrote this cursed letter," I said. "Even the receiver on the desk that monitors Winnie's loft might be explained as a method of protecting her from the stalker, though, of course, that wasn't its original intent. But this note, do you hear, can hang me!"

I touched the flame to the paper. It burned brightly and the smoke carried straight and true up the chimney.

The cat looked at me and winked. Either that or she'd developed a minor tic in her left eye.

37

Linguini's makin' his move late tonight," said Vinnie the following evening, as he laid a shotgun, a baseball bat, and a boning knife on my kitchen counter. "As you can see, we'll be giving him a real welcoming party."

"How can you be so sure he'll make his move tonight?"

"We got our sources. Nobody lies to Joe the Hyena and lives to lie again. Hey! When you gonna start usin' dat fireplace?"

"I've already burned something in it."

"What was it? A fucking twig?"

"An old love letter."

"Fireplaces are good for dat."

"Anything else I need to do to prepare for Linguini?"

"Just have Gena up dere alone by da window where he can see her. As soon as he steps into dat loft and takes out a weapon, we take over."

"Smells good from here," I said.

"Gepetto and a few of da boys are comin' along, too. I recommend clearing de other lesbos out of dere for deir own safety. If you want to be up dere with Gena, it's okay. Just leave dis door unlocked. You may not see us, but we'll be watching you."

"Comforting," I said.

Unlike myself, Vinnie had a few "jobs" to do. He patted the cat and said he'd be dropping in on us later.

"You don't mind I leave some of my stuff here?" asked Vinnie, as he headed for the door.

"No problem," I said.

The cat and I studied the shotgun, the baseball bat—which was wooden, I noticed—and the boning knife. We did not touch any of the items in question. The equipment looked well used.

"Just pray," I said to the cat, "that we don't get caught in the middle of a mob war tonight."

The cat seemed rather cavalier about that possibility. She was much more interested in sniffing the boning knife.

"I seriously doubt," I said, "if that's fish you're smelling."

Around eight o'clock I went up to Winnie's to reconfirm Gena's cooperation and to go over the lighting effects I wanted with Mick Brennan. Mick was already there setting up his lights on the floor beneath the windows that opened onto Vandam Street.

"Now if this bird stands close to the window right about here," said Brennan, "a bloke coming up the street will see her silhouette standing all alone—"

"Exactly like the time Sherlock Holmes set up a silhouette of himself for the gunman across the street."

"Hate to point this out, mate, but Sherlock used a dummy. You've got a gunman coming and you're planning to use a real live girl. Could get a bit dodgy, don't you think?"

"This guy's a jilted lover. He wants to confront his prey first. He's not going to take a shot in the dark from the street. Believe me, it's not his m.o. I'm not worried in the slightest."

"Of course, *you're* not worried, mate. *You're* not going to be standing here in bloody silhouette for the bloke to aim at."

"Please, Watson, please. Your humanity overwhelms me at times. If you'll just handle the lighting, I'll direct the show."

"Break a leg, mate," said Brennan.

By ten-thirty, nerves had been stretched to the limit. Vinnie had gotten word to Rambam, who'd gotten word to me, that Michael Linguini had left his home in New Jersey for the city. If mob sources were accurate, and they usually are, we wouldn't have to be waiting long. That was a good thing, because the only people still remaining at Winnie's studio were Winnie and myself, and the place was starting to feel as big and dark and spooky as an indoor bone orchard.

"Are you sure we need Gena to stand by the window?" asked Winnie with a worried look in her eyes.

"Live bait's the best," I said. "Ask any fisherman."

"I'm asking *your* ass. Is she going to be safe?"

"Safe as walking down the street," I said.

Moments later, as planned, Winnie went across the hallway to Stephanie's apartment to send Gena back by herself. All alone in the dance studio, with Brennan's eerie lighting bouncing off the windows, I reflected very briefly upon what might possibly go wrong. I paced up and down Winnie's loft, waiting for Gena and speaking softly to myself. I missed having the cat to talk to. If anybody'd walked in and found me talking to myself they might've thought I was the mad stalker. As fate willed it, somebody did walk in. And it wasn't Gena.

"Hey, Kinkstah!" said Ratso. "Where is everybody? Where's the girls? Where's the action?"

"Modulate your voice," I said. "Stay away from the lights. What the hell are you doing here?"

"What're you talking about? I'm here for class."

"Does it look to you like there's a class going on here?"

"No. But a moment ago it looked like you were moving your body the way it wanted to. You mean nobody's coming tonight?"

"Yes, Ratso. Somebody's coming. A man bent on murder is coming and he's on his way right now."

"Well, Kinkstah, I'll be leaving then."

"Hold the weddin'. Now that you're here you'd better stay put. The timing's too tight. If you left now and he's just approaching you might spook him."

"He's certainly spooking me."

"Just stay here in the shadows until Gena arrives."

"Gena Lake? The hot redhead? Why is she coming?"

"All in good time, my dear Watson. She's our decoy tonight. The guy in the Lone Ranger mask whom we almost caught last week was once Gena's fiancé. He should be arriving, too, very shortly."

"*He's* coming back? The guy with the gun and the knife?"

"Or the knife and the camera. He likes to change it up every once in a while. Where the hell's Gena?"

By now, I felt sure Vinnie and his guys had taken up their positions, not that I knew where those positions were. Vinnie, like God, was somewhere watching over us. Nonetheless, I worried about the possibility of a mistake. It would be unfortunate if someone like Ratso was wandering around in the hallway and wound up with a boning knife in his back. I just hoped Vinnie's boys knew what they were doing.

Ratso and I were leaning up against the ballet bar when Stephanie walked in. She appeared to be rather highly agitato.

"Gena's not coming," said Stephanie.

"Not coming?" I said. "How can she do this to me?"

"She's having an anxiety attack, you asshole. And it's all your fault."

"You wouldn't want to stand by that window for a while, would you?" I asked politely.

"No," said Stephanie, "but I'll shut it on your dick."

Stephanie made it clear before she stormed back to her apartment that neither she, nor Gena, nor Winnie would be coming out until my little adventure was over and the culprit apprehended. I couldn't say that I truly blamed any of them. But I still needed a silhouette for the stalker. And that really left me with only one choice.

38

"WHAT do you mean you're embarrassed?" I said to Ratso. "You didn't mind wearing the leotard for the girls. Now you're wearing it for a guy. And the red wig from the costume closet is perfect!"

"It's still embarrassing."

"Life is embarrassing, my dear Watson," I said, as I adjusted the wig slightly and turned down the dimmer switch a bit on Brennan's lights. "Death is embarrassing. Making love is embarrassing. Losing love is embarrassing. Watching two dogs hosing on the sidewalk is embarrassing."

"Getting my fucking head blown off would be embarrassing," said Ratso.

"Never happen. This guy wants you to see him before he tries anything. He probably has had a sick little speech echoing around in his desiccated brain for years now. I'll bet he wants to talk to you."

"Well, I don't want to talk to him."

"You won't have to, Watson. He'll never get that close."

"I'll never live this down."

"Rubbish, Watson. This is your finest moment. Your shining hour. Your own personal one-man Camelot."

"I can't stand here any longer."

"Just a few more moments, Watson. I see a light flashing from the building across the street. It may be a signal from our comrades that the villain is entering Vandam Street."

"I can't do it. I've got to take a dump."

"Stand firm, Watson! Stand firm!"

"I have to take a Nixon right now," said Ratso, as he handed me the wig on his rapid way to the dumper. "There are some forces no one can control!"

Ratso taking a Nixon was something you could set your sundial by. He would not be coming back for a long time. Many years, possibly. So I did what I had to do. I threw a shawl around my shoulders, put on the wig, and took Ratso's place by the window.

To be at one with a Sherlockian silhouette was almost a transcendental experience. It might've seemed rather strange to some, even a bit kinky, as it were. Yet, somehow, it felt spiritually right to me, almost as if I were living beyond my bones. One man, standing in the lighted window like an Amsterdam prostitute; wearing a long, itchy, fire-engine-red woman's wig in a deserted lesbian dance studio; standing gentle as the shadow of a woman; standing tall as a wheat field in Kansas.

What happened next happened faster than you fall in love. Out of the corner of my eye I saw the door to Winnie's loft open. A figure wearing a *Phantom of the Opera* mask stepped silently into the room, a gun in one hand, a knife in the other. The figure began to advance stealthily toward me and then hesitated as a baseball bat connected with the back of his head.

In a flash, Gepetto and two guys I'd never seen before were attacking Michael Linguini like human barracuda. It was the kind of thing that could set you off your nice pastrami sandwich. But now there was shouting in the hallway and Vinnie and Rambam came running into the loft. Even Ratso came out to see what was happening.

"Let's hurry it up," said Gepetto. "I got a deposit on the chain saw."

"Hey, Gena!" shouted Vinnie in my direction. "Lose the mustache!"

Soon they had Linguini on his feet. The mask was off and he looked almost handsome in a depraved, delicate, waxen way. But in his dark eyes one could clearly read the dawning dread of the imminent mob justice awaiting him. Without a look back, Vinnie and the boys took him away.

"Jesus," said Rambam. "Did you get a good look at that guy?"

"Yeah," I said. "The face of dead vaudeville."

39

I want to thank all of you for being here," I said, "and for helping to resolve a very dangerous investigation without the loss of a single human life."

"As far as we know," said Rambam rather pointedly.

It was two nights later and I'd invited a highly select group to my loft for a small celebratory party. The guest list consisted of the Village Irregulars and Winnie Katz. Earlier in the day Rambam, to my relief, had disassembled and removed the receiver-phyzagometer apparatus from the loft. We'd decided to leave the pager-transmitter where it was under the sofa in Winnie's studio. By the time somebody discovered it in the year 2017, it'd be an anthropological relic, as would, of course, Rambam and myself.

The affair, unfortunately, had gotten off to a rather unpleasant start when Stephanie had brought in her new one-and-a-half-pound Maltese puppy, Baby Savannah, and the cat had gone right for its throat. We'd barely gotten that situation smoothed over when another altercation broke out, this time between McGovern and Mick Brennan, both of whom had already poured quite a few Guinnesses down their necks.

"*Times* of London won't touch this with a barge pole, mate," said Brennan, as Winnie, I noticed, perked up an ear.

"Bullshit!" shouted McGovern. "I've been in contact with editors over there—"

"Of course, mate. Editors of the bloody tabloids. Tweakin' 'em on the lesbian angle. Sending them girlie shots!"

"The piece is legitimate journalism! The story has legs, I tell you!"

"It bloody well does, mate. Sordid, seamy, same-sex lesbian legs! Bloody beaver close-ups—"

"Let me just mention," I said, stepping in front of the roaring fireplace and trying to put the best face on it, "how grateful I am to both McGovern and Mick for their invaluable assistance in this adventure. McGovern is one of my oldest friends and I'd welcome his involvement as my Watson in future investigations."

"I'm afraid I won't have the time," said McGovern. "This is a rather long article and I'll be asked to write other pieces after that I'm sure."

"And, Mick," I continued, "you've added your expertise and insouciance to the task of assisting me as well. You'd make a fine Watson any time you like."

"Can't do it, mate," said Brennan, as he cheerfully swigged another Guinness. "If McGovern doesn't have time for something, I don't either."

"And how could we conclude this most singular case, without recognizing the contribution of one of my most durable Watsons, Ratso? I know you'll be right beside me, Ratso, the very next time the game is afoot."

"Love to, Kinkstah, but I'll be working on my Abbie Hoffman book. If I have any spare time I'll be doing aerobic workouts at Winnie's. Great potty, though."

"The guilty flee where no man pursueth," I said. "At least there is one man here who is a professional in the field of crime detection. I refer, of course, to Steve Rambam. He's always assisted me in the past, and I know if I call on him in the future, he'll be there."

"Keep dreaming," said Rambam.

"And last, but certainly not least," I said, "is my sleuthing sister-in-crime, Stephanie DuPont. I like to think of the two of us as the Mr. and Mrs. North of the modern era. Of the myriad Watsons who've been of service to me, she may be the most loyal, obedient, and devoted of them all."

The room became very quiet. Stephanie took a small object out of her purse and began doing something with it that created a rather tedious grating noise.

"Do you know what that sound is?" she asked sweetly.

"No," I said. "What?"

"It's the sound your dick is going to make when I put it in this pencil-sharpener."

Fortuitously perhaps, it was that precise moment that Baby Savannah chose to reclaim center stage. McGovern had been sitting in a chair with his legs stretched out just relaxing and drinking a Guinness. Possibly Baby had chosen him because he was there. For whatever reasons have motivated climbers of Mount Everest and young Malteses, her little white fluffy form rapidly propelled itself from McGovern's foot, up one long outstretched leg, into his lap, up his arm, onto his shoulder, and finally, turned to survey her rather awestruck audience from a perch on the very top of McGovern's head. It was a large and comfortable head, apparently, and Baby seemed to be enjoying her new place of residence immensely. It all happened so fast that McGovern had hardly known how to respond. He seemed to be a bit flustered, but also a bit flattered as well.

"Baby Sa*van*nah! Get down!" shouted Stephanie. "You don't know where that head has been!"

"Neither does McGovern," said Brennan.

"Well, I just want to thank all of you," said Winnie, after

things had settled down a bit, "for helping me with my problem. You may not get along with each other all the time, but without you I don't know what I'd have done. You've also provided me with an indelible memory that I'll carry with me for the rest of my life. It was something that I guess I already kind of knew. Just a little thing I happened to see after they beat up that guy."

"Tell us what it was, Winnie," said Stephanie.

Winnie paused for a moment to light a cigarette. Then she blew out the match with a puff of smoke. Then she looked right at me and smiled knowingly.

"It was Kinky wearing that fucking red wig," she said.

40

"Don't take it too hard, Sherlock," said Rambam the next morning, calling, apparently, to give me a little pep talk. "It was a rough-and-tumble adventure. Everybody just needs a little breathing space. They'll get over it. They'll all be back."

"That's what I'm afraid of."

"You'll be happy to know you did garner at least one vote of confidence. Joe the Hyena says your little talk with Gena helped to reconcile the two of them. He says he owes you big time. He's springing not only for the fireplace but for the work on the ceiling as well."

"That's great," I said, as a small piece of plaster fell dangerously close to my cup of espresso.

"And there's one more thing. I got the report back from the graphologist on that threat note."

"You're kidding."

"He says the lack of consistency in the formation of the capital letters is indicative of dangerously erratic mood swings in the subject."

"Okay."

"He says the shaky, poorly defined crossings of the T's indicate a confused sexual identity."

"All right."

"He says loopy, irregular L's and G's are consistent with a long history of drug abuse."

"Okay. Is that it?"

"No. He says the little hat on top of the 'A' is indicative of the fact that the subject was once a country-western guitar picker."

"Okay, Rambam. How'd you know I wrote the note?"

"I overheard you talking to the cat."

"That's impossible. How could you have done that?"

"Simple," he said. "I bugged your loft."

About the Author

A famous detective named Kinkster
Wanted Stephanie so bad that he jinxed her.
When she dumped him at last,
He had just enough gas
To blow out of town on his sphinctster.

—WILL HOOVER